A NURSE IN CONFLICT

A NURSE IN CONFLICT

Gillian Kaye

 CHIVERS

THORNDIKE

This Large Print book is published by BBC Audiobooks Ltd, Bath, England and by Thorndike Press®, Waterville, Maine, USA.

Published in 2005 in the U.K. by arrangement with Robert Hale Limited.
Published in 2005 in the U.S. by arrangement with Robert Hale Limited.

U.K. Hardcover   ISBN 1–4056–3160–0 (Chivers Large Print)
U.K. Softcover   ISBN 1–4056–3161–9 (Camden Large Print)
U.S. Softcover   ISBN 0–7862–7058–6 (Nightingale)

The text of this Large Print edition is unabridged.
Other aspects of the book may vary from the original edition.

Set in 16 pt. New Times Roman.

Printed in Great Britain on acid-free paper.

British Library Cataloguing in Publication Data available

Library of Congress Control Number: 2004111833 ⸮BD

A NURSE IN CONFLICT

CHAPTER ONE

In the ambulance train slowly making its way through France, Laura watched sick with horror as the Stukas dived over a group of villagers and raked them with gunfire. Then she turned away from the pitiful sight on the road which led from the small French village; a few families were in cars having tied a mattress to the roof to try and protect them from the savage machine-gun attacks from the low-flying planes; some were crowded into trucks, but the majority were on foot pushing prams and carts. She saw the sad sight of a very old lady dressed in black being pushed along on a bicycle. At any other time it would have been comical.

Laura had thought of herself as hard, inured to pain and suffering, accustomed to death, but sickness and tears threatened to engulf her as she closed her eyes to the scene outside. Then, as the train started to move again, she turned to find herself looking into the eyes of Dr Kinghorn.

'Sister Terrington . . .' he said, and he gripped her arm.

She felt like flinging herself into his arms to be grasped and comforted, and she almost gave way to her feelings.

But words came to her. 'Dr Kinghorn, they

1

were just village people, I think they were hoping that we would take them on to the train . . . there were children . . . I saw them hit . . .'

'Hush,' he said, his tone stern but not hard-hearted. 'It is war and war is no respecter of age; the innocent and the children are killed as often as our soldiers. But it is our job to heal and not to weep. Come, Sister Terrington, I want you to do some dressings for me.'

Laura was thankful for his words, they steadied her and she followed him slowly and soberly through the train, pulling herself together. I am tired, she was thinking, three nights now with hardly any sleep and there are more injured than we know how to cope with. I chose to be a Queen Alexandra nurse, she said sharply to herself, I could have stayed at home at some safe hospital in England. I wanted to serve at the front, and I'm here, on an ambulance train in the north of France, fleeing the enemy and there is work to be done. By the time she had caught up with the hurrying doctor, she was composed and ready for what she might be asked to do.

For this was the third week in May, 1940; Belgium had fallen, and the ambulance train on which Laura Terrington served was taking its wounded to the northern coast of France. It was a desperate trip. The German army was only hours behind, and the occupants of Laura's train were not the only ones on the

2

move; beside them on the track, they could see the defeated troops of the British Expeditionary Force packed overflowing into trains which were bullet ridden and with shattered windows.

The train was passing slowly through a station as Laura walked to reach her patients; she could see a long line of troops marching away from the small town, and even above the noise of the train, she could hear the low, sinister sound of their heavy boots on the tarmac road.

She reached Dr Kinghorn's side and looked around her at the young soldiers; they were grinning at her.

'Could eat a bit of chocolate, Sister.'

'Haven't got a pint of beer, have you, Sister?'

Their cheerfulness did a lot to dispel the gloom she had been feeling at the plight of the refugees.

'No such luck, boys,' she told them. And I'm sorry to say we're out of bread. The water's a problem, too, until we can fill up and goodness knows when that will be.'

The doctor turned to her. 'I'm told we're getting near Lille,' he said. 'It may be possible to go into the town there and see what we can buy.' He moved away to his next patient and left Laura to her work.

Quickly, Laura changed the dressings on the various injuries; further down the train were the more severely injured who should be moved to hospital, but she could see no chance of that as long as they were in France. The last hospital they had passed at Haubourdin was being evacuated and none of the seriously wounded could be taken from the train.

She was thankful when they reached Lille for they were able to take water on and she and one of her fellow sisters, Jenny Rowbridge, with two of the medical orderlies, walked into the town to do some shopping.

'I feel safer on the train,' said Jenny, as they left the station with the continual sound of gunfire overhead.

Laura agreed with her. 'But it's worth trying to get supplies if we can, we've no idea how much longer we'll be on the train. Are we very far from the coast?'

One of the orderlies seemed to know. 'I think we're about ten miles from Dunkirk. Not very far, but just think how often the line is blocked; it's bloody slow progress.'

They were pleased to be able to buy chocolate, fresh fruit and vegetables, and returned laden to the train.

There, Dr Kinghorn had news for them. 'Try and get some sleep tonight, you two,' he said, looking at Laura and Jenny. 'I've had two medical orderlies from the Casualty Clearing Station in Lille to tell us that we're to take on patients tomorrow afternoon. Then we've got to get the hell out, the gunfire gets nearer

4

every minute.'

'Where are we going?' asked Laura.

'God knows. All I can find out is that every unit in the BEF is retreating to the coast as fast as it can; haven't you seen the troop trains? They're full to overflowing. Let's hope the Navy is there to take us off, that's all.'

Laura looked at him; for a man usually so calm and well-ordered, he was sounding jumpy. He knows more than he's telling us, she thought, and she said no more.

Dr Kinghorn was looking at their bags and sacks of fruit and vegetables, and started to look pleased. 'Take them to Private Georgeson, he'll be glad to see that lot.'

Georgeson was the cook for the train; he had been performing an impossible task with unending swearing and good humour and his good spirits always cheered Laura when she was at her most tired. She and Jenny took him their purchases and each of them got a kiss on the cheek for their efforts.

The medical orderlies from Lille stayed on the train that night and Laura managed to snatch a few hours' sleep; she didn't undress, she hardly had the energy to do so and it didn't really seem to matter.

Next day, they spent the morning getting ready for the intake of patients and when the ambulances started to arrive, all was chaos about them. Bombs began to fall and the train shook and rocked violently, but remained

5

undamaged.

As Laura saw the long line of ambulances, her heart sank for she suddenly realized how difficult it was going to be for them to reach the train; in the end, each stretcher was carried over two railway tracks before being lifted on to the train. Laura thought she had never worked so hard, even at home in Casualty; the men were straight from the Casualty Clearing Station and many of them had nothing more than a first field dressing on their wounds. Overhead, there was a frightening bombardment, but she was too busy to take a great deal of notice or to feel any fear.

As soon as the last of the casualties were on board, the train moved off. Next morning found them stationary on the line, miles from anywhere. As the train came to a halt, Laura stopped what she was doing for a moment and looked over misty fields, and trees in the full leaf of early summer, towards a sleepy French village. The normal life of a French family in its own rural home seemed to be a thing of the past and to have no connection with what she was doing at that moment.

Dr Moorhouse, one of the younger doctors, came into the carriage. 'All right, Sister?' She thought she could detect a note of relief in his voice.

'We're winning,' she smiled.

'We've lost.' His tone was more grim this time. 'We've just heard over the wireless that

6

German troops entered Lille at first light this morning. We only just made it.'

Laura gave a gulp, no wonder Dr Kinghorn had been jittery. 'Will we make it to the coast?' she asked nervously.

'God willing,' he muttered, then tried to sound cheerful. 'I believe we're only about six miles from Dunkirk. Shall I be glad to see the English Channel!' He looked around him. 'Now, what've we got here? Hi, lads, I hope that Sister Terrington has been taking care of you.'

Sister Terrington felt as though she was working like a robot; she had been going from one patient to another all through the night; there were now 350 of them on the train. She was met with pain and with smiles, with jokes and with chatter, but never a grumble; some of the young soldiers seemed no more than lads, all had seen fierce fighting and tried to hide from her the grim remembrance of what they had been through.

The more serious cases were grouped in one carriage; the doctors were in attendance knowing that only the operating theatre would help; and it could be hours, even days, before a hospital was reached.

Laura entered the carriage for the first time to take over from Jenny, who had been there all night.

Her friend looked exhausted.

'Go and lie down, Jenny,' she said, as she

7

took the girl's arm.

Jenny smiled wanly. 'You haven't had any sleep either, Laura. Have you brought the morphine? We need it badly.'

'Yes, I have it and I'm all right. The other boys are all taken care of and a lot of them are sleeping. I'll take over here.'

'Thanks, Laura.' Her companion stopped in the doorway. 'Do you know where we are?' she asked anxiously. 'What is going to happen?'

Laura told her about Lille and that everyone thought that they were only a few miles from the coast.

'Thank God,' Jenny said, and left Laura to her charges.

Laura worked by Dr Kinghorn's side, he seemed untiring. There were many serious injuries and broken bones which he had set with splints in the best way he could. Some of the young men were still unconscious and she went to each one, doing what she could.

She was a tall, slim girl and against the short scarlet cape of the Queen Alexandra's uniform and the white folds of her cap, her hair showed dark in contrast. Her eyes, a soft blue-grey, were serious at that moment; her features, pretty when relaxed, were set in the strain of hours of concentration, making her look older than her twenty-six years. It was her custom to talk to each patient in a soft voice of encouragement and sympathy, treating them all the same and passing from one to another

8

without the time to make any personal recognition or contact with any of them.

So it came with a surprise and shock to her when a few words with the next patient quickened her interest and brought a sense of immediate sympathy and rapport with him. She was sitting with a fair-haired lieutenant still drowsy from his last shot of morphine; his foot had been almost shot away, but Dr Kinghorn had done his best.

As Laura took the young soldier's pulse and found it steady, he opened his eyes and she found herself looking into a gaze which could hardly focus and into eyes as blue as her own.

'Bloody hell.'

'What did you say?' Laura spoke quietly.

His mumbled words became clearer. 'I said "bloody hell". Trust me to meet the most beautiful girl I have ever seen when I'm lying in an ambulance train with a non-existent foot.'

Laura smiled; she was used to remarks like this, but she liked the fair hair and the blue eyes and she liked the courage in his ashen face.

'Can I get you a drink?' she asked him.

'I could do with a whisky, but I don't suppose that's on the cards. Can you manage a cup of tea?'

She nodded and one of the orderlies, hearing the request, went to fetch the drink.

She helped the soldier sit up and kept her

arms around him as he sipped the tea; then he sank back thankfully.

'Saved my life,' he said with a grin, but all the time as he became more alert, she could see the return of the lines of pain to his face.

'Shall I give you another shot of morphine?' she asked him.

'Not for a minute, I want to look at you. Have you got a name?'

'Sister Terrington.'

'Sister Terrington, QA, in your grey and red. I think it must stand for Queen's Angels not Queen Alexandra.'

'Shhh,' she whispered. 'You are talking too much, we don't want you getting a fever.'

'Just tell me where we are,' he said to her. 'They told us we were making for the coast; it's all over in France, isn't it? We were taken to a hospital, but they were in the middle of being evacuated, so I know that things must be pretty bad.'

'We are a few miles out of Lille, but we are not making any progress,' she told him. 'I think we're heading for Dunkirk or somewhere along the coast.'

'There's a note in your voice which tells me that you are hiding something from me. If we are in the middle of nowhere, what is the rumble of guns I can hear in the distance?'

She was serious then. 'The Germans entered Lille early this morning and I think it must be the battle for the town which you can

10

hear . . .'

'Hell, do you mean they are as close as that and we've only just got away in time?' He gave a grimace of pain as he spoke.

She nodded. 'Yes, they were only two hours behind us, I just hope that we're not stuck here for too long. But I want no more talking, your foot is hurting you and I'm going to give you a shot.'

She found her hand suddenly held hard and she returned the clasp for she knew what the next question was going to be.

'Sister, am I going to lose my foot? Will I be able to walk properly again?'

Laura's practical, professional manner returned. 'Your foot might feel very painful, but as soon as we can get you to a hospital, the bones can be set properly and you'll be up in no time. Now stop worrying and go to sleep again.' She met the blue eyes, suddenly friendly and she grinned at him. 'You never know, when you wake up, we might be at the seaside.'

She gave him his injection and he settled down; she thought he seemed more relaxed for the chat. It's all part of nursing, she said to herself; they need to talk as much as they need the morphine, and for a moment, before moving on to her next patient, her eyes rested on the good-looking young face now more peaceful as he slept.

An hour later, the train edged slowly

11

forward. They learned that the line had been blocked by the wing of a fighter which had crashed nearby, but that the driver and stoker of the train had managed to get it clear; mercifully there was no damage to the track.

Dr Kinghorn sent Laura to rest, but she found it hard to sleep; she could hear the bombardment in the distance and overhead there were continuous dogfights which were not alarming, but which made sleeping difficult.

When she woke from what seemed like a troubled doze, she thought that she must have slept the day through and that night had fallen; but a glance at her watch told her that it was three o'clock and when she looked out of the train window she saw that in the distance ahead of them, the sky was black with smoke. She rose hurriedly, wondering where they were and what was happening.

Jenny came in with a cup of tea and a welcome sandwich as she got up, and Laura questioned her friend sharply. 'Where are we, Jenny? What is the smoke?'

They both looked at the pall of thick black smoke and Laura thought that she could pick out bright tongues of flame from all around it.

'It's Dunkirk,' Jenny said. 'They say that the oil tanks have been bombed and are ablaze, but we've got to be prepared to be held up here until we're given the OK to go on. We've been told to get ready to disembark, but we don't know when it will be. That's why I came to wake you up.'

Laura drank her tea hastily and went to get her orders from Dr Kinghorn.

'Make sure that all the walking patients have got their kit-bags ready, Sister Terrington, then come back. I'll need all the help I can get with the stretcher cases. I don't even know if there will be a hospital ship yet; we might have to board whatever can take us across the Channel.'

The train stayed immobile for what seemed like days and they listened with a restless fear to the barrage of gunfire and the deep rumbling explosions of the bombs bursting as they hit the town.

As the train started to creep slowly forward, Laura could not believe the sight in front of her. All along the beach and stretching far across the sand dunes were thousands of troops; some were crouching in the sand, others were waiting in long lines of army khaki. Bombs were falling, but mercifully had little impact as they hit the soft sand.

At the mole nearest to them, boats were lined up to take off as many men as they could and on the sea, which was miraculously calm, there were more waiting. She had expected to see the destroyers of the Royal Navy, she had hoped there would be a hospital ship, but the sight of so many small boats took her breath away.

Some were no more than cabin cruisers or tugs; there were trawlers and fishing craft, barges and pleasure boats all bobbing on the water and awaiting their turn to evacuate the BEF. Some unfortunate ones had been hit and were already ablaze and Laura could see the desperate attempts of their crews to swim to the beach.

She stood in shock, not being able to imagine how they could get their patients safely away. But even thought was taken from her as their OC gave the command for the mobile patients to get off the train and make their way to the east mole. Then it was that Laura knew she had to act.

The troops on the mole were boarding a destroyer and she saw the first of their wounded reach the long line of waiting men; she knew that they would soon be safely aboard. In the stench of burning oil, in the thunderous roar of the Stukas overhead and the bombs falling on the beach, she helped Dr Kinghorn organize the orderlies into stretcher-bearing parties for the severely wounded. How they got them off the train, she never knew, for there was no space to move on the quay and the German attack was concentrated on the wooden part of the sturdy, stone-built mole; if that was destroyed, then no more evacuations could take place even though the boats were ready and waiting.

As the stretcher-party approached the

destroyer, they saw the gangplank go up and the big ship started to move away, making way for an old Thames pleasure boat to come alongside. Laura followed closely and watched as the stretchers were quickly lifted over the side of the small boat, it seemed quicker to do that than to use the gangplank. In no time, the boat was full and all the patients had been taken on; Laura was with the last stretcher and when she had time to look down, she saw that it was the young fair-haired soldier she had spoken to the day before.

'Have we made it, Sister?' he grinned.

She felt she could smile at last. 'I think so,' she said. 'All we've got to do now is avoid the bombs. Jerry is certainly going to try and stop us from getting away.'

Laura was to wish that she had never said those words. The ship they had boarded sailed before the destroyer and she found herself on the deck crouched beside the stretcher; below decks was crammed full to overflowing with many more passengers than the little boat had ever been designed for. As she knelt there, she felt fearful of the bombs which were falling all around them and of being hit by the machine-gun fire from the air. The aerial battle seemed continuous; it was when the firing ceased for a few seconds that the moments of quiet seemed awful and anxious.

With her own eyes, Laura saw the bomb go through the deck; it was only feet away from the stretcher, and she reached out and grasped the soldier's hand and he held on to her. As the bomb exploded below decks, there was an instant inferno; soldiers came up from below, terribly burned and raving with the pain of their burns.

Laura shut her eyes; she imagined this must be the end and she was still clinging to the unknown soldier's hand. Then, amongst the screams, she heard commands and looking up, she saw that the destroyer had drawn alongside them and was lowering rafts to pick up the wounded.

She turned to the young man. 'We've got to jump into the sea or we'll be burned alive. I'll help you.'

'What's your name?'

'Laura.' The reply was automatic, she was busy unfastening the straps that bound him to the stretcher.

'I'm Christopher.'

'Christopher,' she repeated stupidly.

'You go and look after yourself,' he shouted. 'You can't wait for me.'

But Laura had unfastened the straps and was helping him up; he almost fell on top of her, he was so off-balance with his crushed foot.

There was still chaos all round them, the greatest fear being that the boat would blow up; but Laura managed to get Christopher to the rail, helped him up, hung on to him and

16

then jumped with him before she had time to think about what she was doing.

In the water, he managed better and she started swimming alongside him while he struck out strongly with his arms, dragging his injured foot behind him. The raft seemed a long way off.

Laura had never been a good swimmer and she could feel herself failing; her lungs were bursting, her arms felt as though they had no strength in them.

'You go on,' she gasped. 'I'm done for.'

The water washed over her head and desperately she tried to struggle to the surface again, each movement of her arms getting more and more feeble until she thought that she was going to be sucked down. Then she felt a hand clutch her shoulder and she was conscious of the strength of her companion as he kept her going; her head was above water again and seconds later, willing hands were helping them on to the raft.

Everything went hazy to Laura after that; she felt herself hauled up on to the destroyer and once again she was lying on a deck, this time soaking wet and shivering, but still alive. Her companion, who had called himself Christopher, was missing.

She never knew how many were rescued from the old Thames pleasure boat, it blew up a few moments later. She was helped below decks on the crowded destroyer and someone took her to a tiny empty cabin; a pair of thick trousers and a shirt were thrust into her hand and she had enough sense and strength to get out of her wet things and put on the dry, rough garments; she kept on her wet stockings and shoes and bundled up her uniform, tying it together with her belt.

'I'm alive,' she cried out. 'I'm alive.' Then tears trickled down her face as she remembered all her poor patients from the train who had perished in the small boat.

Then she remembered the young man who had got her through the water and went in search for him. After an hour of wandering around in a daze, she knew she would have to give up looking for him; he was not to be found anywhere, though her task was difficult as it was almost impossible to move on the crowded vessel. She felt saddened, as he had helped her those last yards to the raft when her strength was failing and she was so sure he had made it to the destroyer in safety.

She did have the joy and relief of finding Jenny and the other sisters who had boarded the destroyer in front of her; they were already at work in the sick bay, but she did not come across Dr Kinghorn or any of those who had been the first to go below on the pleasure boat.

She went back on deck and found that it was beginning to get dark. Behind them lay the red glow which was the burning Dunkirk; around them the countless small boats bobbed and tossed as they travelled to and fro across the Channel; overhead, the gunfire continued. The deck was crowded, everyone looking their last at the French coast and risking the bombardment from above, the mood amongst the men mixed, for in their minds they knew defeat. The enemy had chased them out of France, many of their number had died, even more had been wounded, but they had escaped and lived to fight another day in whatever way their country should ask of them.

All these thoughts raced through Laura's mind and she decided that it would be sensible to go back down below. As she made her way through the mass of soldiers on the deck, she heard her name being called.

'Laura!'

She looked around from one soldier to another and thought she must have imagined the sound.

'Laura, I'm here.'

Then she saw him; or rather, she saw a great pile of lifebelts and propped up against them with a white face under a steel helmet and engulfed by a great trench-coat, was Christopher.

She was at his side and clutching at his hands. 'I didn't think you'd made it,' she gasped. 'I've been looking for you everywhere and . . . and . . .' She felt the sobs rising in her throat, the tears pouring down her face.

'Hang on,' he said, as his eyes searched her

face and he cradled her hands in his. 'The pleasure boat blew up, didn't it? Were we the only ones to get off?'

She gulped hard and dashed her hand against her eyes. 'There are so many with bad burns; some of them made it, they jumped over the side when we did and the rafts picked them up. They are being treated down in the sick-bay, but I can't find Dr Kinghorn or any of our orderlies who went below before the bomb struck us. I think we've lost them all. I should be used to things like this by now, but it seems so tragic when we were just getting away.'

He was still gripping her hands. 'But all the patients who could walk and came on the destroyer, are they all right? And the other sisters?'

'Yes, I found them organizing the sick-bay, and that reminds me, what about your foot? Did your dressings survive the water? And what have you got on under that ridiculously large trench-coat?'

'Don't you laugh! You don't look like a fashion model yourself. I've still got my wet clothes on so at least the coat is keeping me warm. I don't know who gave it to me. And I daren't look at my foot, it's giving me hell.'

She knelt beside him and found a few shreds of wet bandage covering his injured foot. Then she looked up at him, his face seemingly the one familiar thing in this nightmare world. 'I'll go to the sick-bay and organize a stretcher for you; they'll see to your foot and find you some dry clothes.'

She left him and hurried back to the sick-bay, falling over kit-bags, stepping carefully over sleeping soldiers and finding, on the way, two sturdy gunners who said they would get a stretcher for her.

It took an hour to move Christopher, get him stripped and dried, his wound dressed, and lying as comfortably as he could on the floor in the small room which was the destroyer's sick-bay. Laura propped herself up against him, someone brought them mugs of tea, sweet and strong, and the hot drink improved their spirits.

She still felt sick and shaken by what had happened, not being able to believe that her brave, sensible Dr Kinghorn had gone. She had worked with him and the orderlies on the ambulance train for three months and they had been bombarded many times, but each time they had come off lightly. Now she knew that it had been a trick of fate that she had been last on board the old pleasure boat with Christopher and that they had got no further than the deck. It had saved their lives.

She was exhausted, but her troubled thoughts kept her awake; they were well clear of Dunkirk and making good headway across the Channel. Darkness had fallen and all over the ship, weary and wounded soldiers slept wherever they could find a space. Laura thought that she must be the only one awake; after the tumult of Dunkirk, the occasional aircraft overhead did little to break the quiet.

Christopher dozed at her side, but as first light appeared and she thought that they must be nearing Dover, she felt a hand on her shoulder.

She looked up. 'Are you all right?' she asked him.

'Yes, thank you. I just want to say something in case we never meet again. You saved my life, Laura, I shall never forget. If you hadn't got me over the side of that boat, I'd have gone up with the rest of them, poor buggers.'

She gave a little smile. 'I think that it was you who saved *my* life; I couldn't have swum another stroke, yet somehow you got me on to that raft. I shall never forget it either.' She stood up then and took a look at him. 'I'll stay with you and get you to the hospital when we reach Dover. I don't think it will be long now.'

It was, in fact, many hours later before they were able to disembark. Ships, large and small, were queuing up at the entrance to the port as the thousands of troops went ashore. It was well organized, but the massive problem of moving that number of personnel by train and army lorry was almost insurmountable.

Long before they reached the coast, the whole of the intake of the troops on the destroyer crammed on to the decks to get the first glimpse of the white cliffs. From where she was below, Laura could hear the excitement in their voices, the songs, the relief and joy of being safely home.

Then it was their turn to go alongside the quay; she went to have a look for herself and could see lines of army trucks waiting at the quayside and a row of ambulances. She and Jenny got the stretcher-bearers together to take the most badly injured of the men, and then she decided to hang back and wait until the crush was over.

She was determined to stay with Christopher, for she could feel the bond that had formed between them in those frightening minutes when the steamer was bombed and they had found themselves in the water.

They chatted together until it was their turn to get into the ambulance to be taken to an overcrowded hospital which was doing its best with the influx of patients. She knew she looked a sight in her khaki shirt and trousers, but she had lost everything; quickly, she handed Christopher over, telling him she would come and look for him later.

She found a sister in charge and explained that she was a QA and that they had been bombed at sea; she still clutched her sodden uniform. A young nursing student sent the bundle to the laundry, then took her to the nurses' home, showed her the bathroom, laid out a uniform, and told her she could make tea and some toast in the nurses' kitchen when she wanted something to eat. She could lie on the nurse's bed until she felt better.

The bath was bliss; Laura could not imagine anything more wonderful than the blessing of the hot water on her aching body. She borrowed some talcum powder, put on the fresh clean uniform, lay down on the bed and slept.

As she struggled awake, hours later, Laura thought she was still in the water and she felt again that sense of having to give way and let the seas close finally over her head. Then she made herself remember the grip on her shoulder from an unknown wounded man called Christopher, and she opened her eyes and tried to visualize his face with a sense of gratitude and pleasure.

She got up slowly; she knew she must report to her London office, but suddenly food was of the first importance and she made her way to the nurses' kitchen. She found bread and butter and a gas stove, and a tin of baked beans, and she had never enjoyed beans-on-toast so much in all her life. She also made coffee, which seemed a luxury, but she rationed herself to just one of the nurses' biscuits.

Then she went in search of Christopher. The discipline in this overcrowded hospital was incredible, she found; there were many wards with mattresses put down between the beds and there were lines of beds along the corridors, but all was orderly and there did not seem to be a shortage of nurses.

She found him at last in men's surgical, or what she found was his empty bed. The name on the bedhead said Christopher Leybourne, and the notes described his injured foot. She waited until a nurse came by and she was told that he was in the operating theatre. Laura went in search of Sister, explained the situation and was told, yes, she could wait until he returned from theatre and she could also use the office telephone to ring QA headquarters whenever she wanted to.

Laura decided to ring London straight away so that she could be at Christopher's side when he came round. The telephone line was dreadful and it took a quarter of an hour to get through. But she spoke to one of the senior staff and was told that under the circumstances, she should rest as much as she could, take two weeks' leave and report for duty on 15 June.

Back on the ward, she didn't feel guilty sitting by the bed for she knew that she was releasing one of the young nurses who would have been stationed there when Christopher came back from theatre. No one took any notice of her; the occupants of the beds near her were either asleep or heavily sedated.

The theatre trolley was wheeled through and Christopher transferred to his own bed. She sat looking at his still face and felt a sudden sense of familiarity. She had known him for little more than three days, had exchanged no more than a few words with him, yet he had somehow become an urgent and integral part of her present life; she found the feeling strange, but comforting.

She was used to the different reactions of patients coming out of an anaesthetic and knew that he could rave and talk rubbish to her, he could just open his eyes and then pass into a natural sleep, or he could be very sick.

But what she had not expected was that he should wake up an hour later, turn his head to look into her eyes and utter her name. 'Laura.'

'Christopher.' She put her fingers on his pulse.

He looked around him. 'Christ, where am I? I thought for a moment that I was at Hayle and you were there with me.'

She spoke quietly. 'You were injured and brought to my ambulance train, then we were evacuated from Dunkirk and got bombed. Do you remember? This is a hospital in Dover; I brought you here.'

His eyes were starting to droop again. 'Thank God you are here. I'll be all right now.' And he slept.

Laura touched his hand, went in search of the staff nurse and told her that he was sleeping naturally. She was feeling hungry and wondered if she dared go in search of the nurses' dining-room and beg something to eat.

And she had to decide what to do; she couldn't stay here indefinitely.

She ate a good meal and felt better; as she sipped her coffee afterwards, she decided that she would try and find a bed for the night, and then she would have to borrow some money somehow, retrieve her uniform and make her way back to London. She must make up her mind whether to go and say goodbye to Christopher or to treat their brief and life-saving relationship as just one of wartime's strange and transitory meetings.

When Laura reached the bedroom where she had slept so well, she found the young nurse just coming off duty.

'Hello,' she said. 'Thanks for the loan of your bed, it saved my life.'

'You looked all in,' was the reply. 'Were you at Dunkirk? We've heard some terrible stories and yet so many escaped, it seemed like a miracle.'

Laura nodded. 'It was a hell-hole, but thousands got away. Those small boats were incredible; I was on an old Thames pleasure-boat, but it was bombed . . .' To her horror, her eyes filled with tears and the fear and sickness returned. 'I'm sorry, I don't think I can talk about it yet. I'm lucky to be alive.'

Sympathetic eyes looked into hers. 'I'm sorry, I shouldn't have mentioned it. I've got your uniform back, you're a QA, aren't you? Have you been in France?'

'Yes, on an ambulance train. I didn't mind that, though it was hairy at times, made you wonder if you'd been mad to go out there when you could have been safe at home. I wouldn't have missed the experience, but I don't know where I'll be sent next.'

The young nurse smiled, she looked tired. 'It's pretty hairy here, too,' she said. 'There are air raids every night and these last few days we've been working all hours; I'm ready for bed right now. What are you going to do?'

Laura frowned. 'I'm planning to go back to London in the morning. Do you think you could find me a bed? Have you got a friend who's on night duty?'

'Yes, of course, you can have Sally's room, it's only just across the corridor; she's just gone on duty. I'll show you; here's your uniform.'

Laura smiled her thanks and said goodbye; she settled down in yet another bed and slept soundly through the night for the first time in months.

Next morning, she was glad to put on her own uniform again and make her way to the dining-room for breakfast. She had tried not to think too much about Christopher, but before she went off to see the almoner about a travel warrant, she knew she must come to some decision about him.

Some deep instinctive feeling was telling her that she mustn't lose touch with him; it was something more than the bond that the saving of their lives had brought about. She had felt attracted to him as soon as she had seen him on the train and could not bring herself to leave the hospital without at least saying goodbye to him. Just see him once more, she was saying to herself, then they could go on into the war in their own separate ways. She didn't know what it was that was making her hesitate, but thought perhaps that she felt a little frightened of an emotional farewell.

She had to wait a long time to see the almoner, but got a cheery reception; there was no trouble over the warrant for the train and she was given five pounds to help with the journey and to buy whatever she needed.

It was the middle of the morning before she made her way to the surgical ward and when she reached Christopher's bed, she received a pleasant surprise. For he was sitting up, shaved, his fair hair combed neatly back, and looking years younger. He also looked worried.

She called his name as she reached the bed. 'Christopher, is something wrong? You look worried.'

His head turned quickly in her direction, his brow cleared and his hand reached out to hers.

'Laura, thank God. I thought you'd gone without coming to say goodbye and I couldn't bear it.' He gripped her hand fiercely and looked at her with a smile. 'And you are in your scarlet and grey again, you look lovely.'

She didn't even admit to herself how very nearly she hadn't come, for she suddenly felt that she was in the right place, sitting at his side, her hand in his.

'You are looking a lot better. How is your foot?'

He grinned and pointed to the cradle over his leg, keeping the bedclothes from touching his foot. 'I don't know what they did, but it's feeling a lot better and they say I can get up and start trying to walk with crutches as soon as I feel strong enough. You nurses are bloody marvellous, I shall never forget it.'

'It's our job and we love it,' she said. 'Which reminds me, they've given me two weeks off before I'm sent somewhere else, so I'm going back to London later this morning.'

His hand gently brushed her cheek and the gesture brought a flush to her face. 'Laura, I can't bear to let you go, I've only just met you.'

She met the deep blue of his eyes in a searching gaze and the look she saw there held all the emotion she had been hoping to avoid.

'Laura,' he said softly. 'I think I've fallen in love with you.'

CHAPTER TWO

For long moments, Laura looked at Christopher; then she glanced round the ward.

At least fifty men, some seriously wounded, others with broken limbs; all around her the ruined humanity which was war, and in the middle of it a declaration of love.

She put out a hand towards the young man, for she knew that she, too, had grown attached to him, but to herself she could not use the word 'love'.

'Christopher,' she said, and tried to laugh light-heartedly, 'you don't know me; we've hardly met and we don't know anything about each other.'

He was holding her hand very tightly. 'None of that seems to matter, Laura. I was drawn to you straight away in the train, but might never have seen you again. But fate threw us together; it threw us into the sea and I cannot forget your face, your bravery. Don't disappear into the blue, my dear girl; at least tell me your name and where to find you so that when I am mobile again, I can come and look you up.' He stopped, seeing a frown come into her face. 'What is it, Laura? You have just thought of something unpleasant.'

She shook her head. 'No, it's not unpleasant, it's just duty. I've got to report to my unit at the end of the month and I just don't know where I shall be sent. We have to be prepared to go anywhere.'

'I know all that,' he replied. 'I shall be going back, too, once I'm passed fit. We've been run out of France, but that's not the end of it and I shall fight wherever they send me. Don't you see, Laura, that's why we've got to make the most of every minute God sends. Tell me about yourself quickly, for soon this foot of mine will begin to play up and I shall get tetchy. Stay with me for a little while.'

How could she refuse? He seemed so young and vulnerable, but Laura knew that it was more than pity she felt for him.

'I'm Laura Terrington,' she said gently. 'I'm twenty-six and I've been nursing since I left school. I was a reserve in the QAs and was sent to France as soon as the war started.'

'And you're not engaged or anything, not attached to anyone?'

She shook her head. 'No, there seems to have been little time for romance, or maybe I've not met the right person or something like that.'

'Perhaps you've met him now!' he said, and there was a cheeky grin on his face.

'Oh, Christopher, please don't rush me. Tell me something about yourself. Where is your home?'

'I am Christopher Leybourne, twenty-five years of age. I am a junior partner with a firm of solicitors in Richmond in Yorkshire and that is where my home is. Like you, I was sent to France at the end of last year.' They both laughed at his matter-of-fact tone and then he asked her rather anxiously, 'Where are you going to stay when you are in London, Laura?'

'I share a flat with my sister Dorothy in Bayswater; she is a teacher and she has been evacuated with her school into Somerset, so I will have the flat to myself for the time being.'

'Will you write down the address for me, and are you on the phone?'

It was Laura's turn to grin. 'Do you realize that I haven't got a thing except the clothes I stand up in? You haven't either. I'll go and beg a pencil and some paper from Staff, if she's not too busy.'

She walked the length of the ward and knew that Christopher's eyes were on her; she thought of his words and wondered if he would say anything more before she left. They exchanged addresses and promised to keep in touch with each other, though Christopher admitted to being a bad correspondent, preferring the telephone as a means of communication. Laura seemed to think that he would be sent on to a quieter hospital once they were satisfied that his foot was on the mend.

She stood by the bed, holding on to his hands; she felt a pang on leaving him and was suddenly at a loss for words; then Christopher whispered something and she had to bend her head to try and catch what he was saying.

His mouth near her cheek, she heard the soft words. 'Would you kiss me goodbye, Laura?'

It took only a slight turn of the head for

their lips to meet. 'Laura, I love you,' he murmured. 'Please don't forget me and let's hope that the war won't separate us for too long.'

She straightened up and smiled. 'Let me know where they send you, Christopher, and I will write to you. And if there is anything you need, I can send it from London. Goodbye and God bless you.'

'Goodbye, Laura.'

She left him then and hurried down the ward, trying to still the swift beat of her heart; his kiss had disturbed her more than she dared admit to herself.

She left the hospital and walked quickly through the town to the railway station, stopping at a small gift shop to buy herself a light shopping bag and purse.

When she saw the station, Laura nearly cried out in dismay, for outside were trucks full of soldiers being brought from the boats and there was a queue of a hundred yards long and four deep to get on to the platform. It didn't seem a remote possibility that anyone would get away that day. She didn't see one female face in all that huge crowd, but the soldiers she stood with were cheerful and encouraging.

'Hello, Sister, you hoping to get to London? Where's your baggage then?'

She told the young Cockney corporal how she had lost everything; he was kindly and sympathetic.

'You was unlucky then, catching a bomb like that. We thought we'd had it once, but it missed us by inches, the bugger. Begging your pardon, Sister. We were on a trawler, didn't 'alf stink of fish, but what was that when we were on our way home to ol' Blighty?' He eyed her up and down. 'Look, Sister, you stick alongside o' me when our turn comes, I'll see you safe on the train. Don't want you getting crushed in the crowd, not after what you been through.'

He was one of the best tonics Laura could have had; his name was Alf and he went on talking without stopping until it was time to board the train. He found her a seat and then stood in front of her as though he was determined to protect her at all costs. Arriving in London, he wouldn't leave her until he had seen her safely on the bus which would take her to Bayswater. When he said goodbye to her, she reached up and kissed his cheek and told him that she would never forget him.

On the bus, she realized that she had meant her words; he was the typical British soldier with all the grit and humour and cheerful common sense which his country was going to need in the days to come.

Laura got out of the bus at the end of Peel Street and called at the corner shop which she and Dorothy always used.

Mrs Dornford, the shopkeeper, greeted her

ecstatically. 'Sister Terrington, we thought of you when they began taking them off from Dunkirk; we guessed you was in France. Thank goodness you're safe.'

Laura explained how she had lost all her belongings and asked what she could buy without a ration book.

'Now, Sister, you're not to worry about that. You can share ours, you just give me your bag and I'll fill it up with everything you'll need when you get in your flat. A good rest is what you'll be wanting.'

'Thank you, Mrs Dornford, you're a gem. I'll go and see about my ration book tomorrow.'

Laura walked down the street wondering if London had yet suffered any air-raids; all seemed strangely quiet and orderly after the chaos of the past few days. The Victorian terraced houses of the street had an air of dignity and a reassuring look of permanence; the trees down one side of the road were in the fresh leaf of early summer and were untouched by smoke and bomb-blast. Laura marvelled; was it possible that she was walking down a quiet London street that was home, with a bag full of food and necessities and that, in minutes, she would reach the sanctuary of her flat?

Laura and Dorothy shared a flat on the top floor of a tall villa; the entrance was shabby but clean, and as she went in, Laura was engulfed by the feeling of a safe homecoming; she felt tears come into her eyes. She set off up the stairs and hadn't gone more than six steps when she stopped abruptly; how on earth was she going to get in? She had no key, nothing.

Then she turned to go down again as she remembered old Mrs Hancock in the bottom flat; they had always left a spare key with her in case they locked themselves out.

She knocked sharply on Mrs Hancock's door, and to her relief heard a shuffling step and the bolt being drawn back, then the door opened.

The little lady was no more than five feet tall and as round as a barrel; Laura had always imagined that Queen Victoria must have looked just like that in her later years. Mrs Hancock always wore black, too, in memory of her husband who had been killed in the last war. Now, just over twenty years later, she was more than seventy, but alert and self-sufficient.

She looked at Laura, puzzled for a moment, and then a smile lit up her face.

'Sister Terrington! Miss Laura, come in, come in. You're back at last and safe, too. How I've worried about you and committed you to the good Lord every night. And now you're home, safe and sound. Come in and I'll make you a cup of tea. Where's your case?'

'Oh, Mrs Hancock, it's lovely to see you. I got bombed escaping from France and I've lost everything. Mrs Dornford from the shop has stocked me up with food, but I forgot I couldn't even get into the flat. Have you still got our spare key?'

'Of course I have, in a safe place, too. Now, are you going to come in and have a cup of tea with me?'

'Thank you very much, but I won't stop now. I've gone so many nights without sleep that all I can think about is bed. I will come and see you tomorrow.'

'You do just that,' the old lady replied. 'Just as well it's warm weather, at least your flat won't be cold, just needs a good airing. I kept my eye on it last winter for you, we didn't have any bursts.'

'Thank you, Mrs Hancock, I'll go on up now.'

Laura took the key and quickly climbed the stairs. She opened her door and looked around; sitting-room, a bedroom each, kitchen and bathroom, how lovely it all looked. It was home, she thought. And she put her bag on the bed and lay down and wept. She cried until all the tensions, all the sadnesses had gone; she cried for her young wounded soldiers, she cried for dear Dr Kinghorn, she cried for the poor burned souls in the Thames pleasure-boat, she cried until she could cry no more.

Then she lay there and looked around her, all so comfortable and familiar: the flowered curtains, the soft green carpet and the old gleam of the mahogany wardrobe and dressing-table.

Perhaps I needed to cry, she said to herself as she got up from the bed, I'll be all right now.

She unpacked the shopping bag and nearly cried again when she saw what Mrs Dornford had put in. She knew that there was black market food about, but she hadn't expected a tin of ham and a tin of peaches along with the necessary items of bread, milk, butter, eggs and sugar.

She made a meal for herself and felt better afterwards; she switched the wireless on for the nine o'clock news and was in time to hear that Mr Churchill had been speaking of the evacuation from Dunkirk in the House of Commons:

'. . . we must be careful not to assign to this deliverance the attributes of a victory. Wars are not won by evacuations.'

Laura listened very carefully and then heard words which sent a thrill of pride through her and made her feel that what she had been through had not been in vain:

'. . . we shall fight in the seas and the oceans, we shall fight with growing confidence and growing strength in the air; we shall defend our island whatever the cost may be. We shall fight on the beaches, we shall fight on the landing-grounds, we shall fight in the fields and in the streets, we shall fight in the hills; we shall never surrender . . .'

He's right, she said to herself, with tears in her eyes; all those thousands of soldiers who went home from Dover will go on fighting. That nice London corporal on the train, he was typical of all our troops. They will fight, just as Mr Churchill says, they won't surrender.

The next day, she would have a lot to do, so she quickly washed up, put a hot-water bottle in the unused bed and got herself off to sleep early. She woke at first light, but it did not worry her. She had a lot of thinking to do and before she started to make her plans, she thought of Christopher. She wondered, in the first place, if she would ever see him again; already the incident was fading into the past and she knew that it would be easy for him to forget her. She had liked him so much, but had been a little alarmed at the intensity of his feelings for her; only time would tell.

Now she must get down to practicalities; first to go to the Food Office, then to QA headquarters to see if they had pay for her; she had to have something to live on, though she knew her parents would be willing to lend her money.

Laura's home was in Cumberland; she and her sister had been born and educated in

London, but when her father had retired as headmaster of a big London school, he and Mrs Terrington had decided that their London home was too big for them with both daughters living elsewhere. They had always spent their holidays near Penrith and had decided to move to a small cottage near the town; they never regretted the move and Laura often visited them. It would be wonderful to spend a week or two up there, she thought, and made up her mind to phone them that evening.

She knew she must get in touch with Dorothy, too. Her sister would be relieved to know that she was home and Laura guessed that she would be pressed to pay her a visit in Somerset.

The next day was a busy one and she found that she tired easily; there was money waiting for her at headquarters and she was told that she would be sailing on the *Queen Mary* on 29 July, but to report for her orders a week before that. It gave her nearly two months to recover, to visit Penrith, and perhaps to go and see Dorothy for a few days.

She spent some time shopping in Oxford Street, buying all the personal things she had lost from her kit and, on the way home, she stopped again at Mrs Dornford's and bought enough in the way of essential foods to stock up the larder at the flat.

She walked back along Peel Street, satisfied

with her day's work and reached the flat ready to put her feet up and try to relax a little. She slept for an hour and when she woke up, she found herself thinking again of Christopher; the memory of the fair-haired young soldier did not seem to go away. His words of love had been spoken in the stress of the moment and much as she would have liked to have known him better, she told herself firmly to put him out of her mind. Nothing could be certain in wartime and it was better not to foster hopes of something which might never come to pass.

The next few weeks went by very pleasantly, and Laura began to feel relaxed and able to put the harrowing events of Dunkirk behind her. There were no air raids over mainland Britain, and she visited both Cumberland and Somerset. There, she found Dorothy newly married to a teacher who had fought in Belgium and had then been invalided out of the army; he had returned to his old school and to Dorothy and they had married without telling anyone.

In the Lake District, her parents were relieved to see her looking so well and she was glad to walk in the wide open spaces again; her mother spoiled her and would not let her do any of the cooking. Eggs and cheese were easily come by in the country, and to Laura it was a different world from the one she had experienced in the previous six months.

Back in London after her two visits, Laura

had several weeks before she had to report for her orders and before she was due to sail. She felt restless after the calm of her holiday and found herself with a sense of disappointment that she had heard nothing from Christopher. He must have regretted his hasty declaration, she said to herself, unless he has been ill; the anxious thoughts about him added to her restlessness and she tried to forget about him, wishing it was time to be on her way and busy and involved again.

She spent the days walking in Hyde Park, strolling down Oxford and Regent Street or sitting quietly in the flat with a book from the public library. Returning from Mrs Dornford's shop quite early one morning, she was puzzled to see someone standing on the steps of the house in Peel Street.

As she got nearer, her heart missed a beat for she saw that it was a man and that he was holding a stick.

Christopher.

She ran the length of the last few houses, arriving laughing and out of breath at his side. He dropped the stick and she was in his arms, caught up in a kiss of desperate longing and intense in its search for her love. She returned it and then broke away to look at him.

'Oh, Christopher, Christopher, what are you doing here? Where have you been? And you look so brown!'

With his arms around her shoulders, he

looked into her eyes. 'So many questions, my darling, darling Laura. I was so afraid that I would find you gone, but your little neighbour on the ground floor told me that you were still here, so I've not been waiting long. We've got so much to talk about, Laura, but first things first. I've come to ask you something special, can we go up to your flat to talk?'

She looked at him; he was dashing, handsome and he looked so young, though she knew he was only a year younger than herself. A bubble of excitement burst in her and she reached up to kiss him again.

Going up the steps to the front door, she turned to him. 'Christopher, your foot, how is it? We've got two flights of stairs.'

He smiled. 'Those doctors are magicians; my foot is as good as new though it does get stiff.'

He followed her in and Mrs Hancock appeared at the foot of the stairs.

'Miss Laura, you've come home. I told the gentleman that you wouldn't be long. Is he your young man?'

Trying to be serious, Laura made the introductions and Christopher made Mrs Hancock's day by bending over and kissing her on the cheek. 'Yes, I hope I am her young man, Mrs Hancock, she wasn't gone long, was she?'

He was slow and careful as he climbed the stairs, but Laura did not attempt to help him;

it seemed a miracle to her that his foot had mended so quickly.

Inside the flat, Christopher took her in his arms again. He held her as though she were a precious piece of porcelain; something to be valued and treasured. He said very little, seeming to have something on his mind. Laura, full of curiosity, did not probe too deeply. She made coffee for them both and then sat by his side on the settee, happy to be in his presence and not wanting to force confidences from him if he did not want to make them. In the end, it all came from Christopher and she did not have to ask.

'I was terrified that you would have been sent off somewhere again,' he said. 'I expect you are wondering why I didn't write to you. I'm sorry, that's all I can say, I don't know if I can make you understand.'

'Don't worry,' she replied. 'I suppose I was disappointed in a way, but I had to tell myself that our meeting was unconventional to say the least of it; you might have regretted what you said that last time we were together.'

He groaned. 'Laura, I kept thinking that I must have made a fool of myself. Within a couple of days, I was transferred to a hospital at Barmouth in west Wales; that's where the doctors performed their magic. In days, I was walking along the sea front—that's why I look so brown—and I couldn't believe how quickly my foot healed. The bones are still mending,

45

but it's discomfort rather than pain that I feel now.'

He paused and took her hand tightly between both of his. 'But I don't want to talk about that. I have to tell you that I'm sorry I didn't write to you. I had your address safely and I hadn't forgotten about you, but I'd told you that I wasn't good at writing letters. By the time I got to Barmouth and started to recover, I began to wonder if I'd imagined the scene in the hospital. I knew I'd fallen in love with a nurse called Laura, that she'd saved my life and got me safely back home, but I could not remember what I'd said to you. It was as though I was still in shock. So I dared not write, I didn't know what to say; you could have forgotten me. It wasn't until I reached London last night that all my doubts disappeared and I knew I had to seek you out.'

He bent forward and his lips gently touched her forehead, her cheeks and then her mouth. 'As soon as you started running towards me down the street, I knew that everything was real. Now we are here together.'

Laura smiled at him. 'I thought you must have regretted saying what you did about loving me. You see, on the train, I got used to soldiers saying that they loved me, it almost became a joke. But something kept telling me that this time it wasn't a joke.'

Christopher shook his head. 'No, it wasn't a joke, Laura, I do love you and I want to ask you something special.'

His face suddenly became more serious and Laura knew that she was going to learn what he had been keeping from her ever since he had arrived.

'Laura, how much longer have you got of your leave?'

'Nearly a month,' she answered. 'I sail on 29 July.'

'Thank God,' he said quietly. 'I've arrived in time. I want to ask you, Laura, if you will marry me. I love you very much and would like to be married to you more than anything else in the world.'

Laura was not shocked, but she was stunned. She hardly knew him, but she could feel that she would come to love him. But marriage? It was not something to be undertaken in a rush, but the war seemed to have made it necessary to make decisions like this almost without pausing to think about it.

The silence hung between them, thoughtful, meaningful, but not uneasy.

'Are you going to say yes, Laura? I feel so certain of your love and we would be very happy, I am sure of it.'

Laura looked at him; she saw the love in his eyes, but at that moment did not know if she could return it. She was attracted to him, she knew, but how would one recognize love in such circumstances? Love in wartime was transient. It had a fleeting, elusive quality which at some moments seemed within reach and yet in the very next minute could seem unattainable.

Laura was lost in thought and when Christopher's arm came round her shoulders and his hand tilted her face to his, it came with almost a surprise that he was there at all.

'What are you thinking, Laura? You're not sure, are you?' Then his voice became urgent. 'Let me show you that I love you, Laura, please say yes to me.'

She hid her face against his jacket, liking the rough feel of the tweed; it was something solid and real and she suddenly knew what her answer was going to be.

'Yes, Christopher,' she whispered. 'I would like to marry you.'

He kissed her then and Laura felt the first moments of love and magic. 'Oh, Christopher,' she whispered. 'I really do think that I love you, but we will have to wait until after the war, won't we?'

'Wait?' He laughed and hugged her to him. 'I thought we could go to the Registry Office or the church and get married tomorrow; I did get permission from my CO and I think you'd better do the same from your QA people.'

'Stop, Christopher, stop!' She was laughing, too. 'You can't get married just like that unless it's by special licence and you have to get that from a bishop or someone.'

'Do you mean we have to get the banns

called?'

She nodded. 'Yes, that's right, they have to be called for three weeks at a church service in the parish where the couple live; and you don't even live in this parish.'

'Are you making difficulties, my darling girl?'

'No,' she protested, 'I'm being practical. Can you get the banns called at your church? I think you said it was in Richmond in Yorkshire.'

He was suddenly serious. 'No, I am not going to tell the family yet. I want to slip away and marry you quietly all on our own. Do you have a church near here, Laura?'

'Yes, it's St Barnabas, just down the bottom of the next street. I always go there when I am at home.' Laura was getting used to the idea that Christopher really did want to marry her, though it puzzled her a little why he did not want to tell his family.

He smiled. 'That's fine. I will give this flat as my address and we can go and see your vicar and ask him to call the banns, then we can be married in three weeks' time; that will be just before you have to sail. We will be married and I'll try and borrow a car and take you to a little place I know down by the Thames at Marlow. There is one snag though, Laura, that I have not told you about.'

'What is that?'

'I have been posted for training for three

weeks; Salisbury Plain of all places. I think it's to make sure that my foot is ready for active service.'

Laura stared at him. 'Christopher Leybourne, are you telling me that you want us to arrange to have the banns called for our wedding, then you go away for three weeks and I shan't see you; then we marry and two days later I sail off in the *Queen Mary*?'

Christopher laughed aloud. 'You are exactly right; it's called a wartime marriage! But we love each other and we will have two blissful days at Marlow before we have to be parted. Come along, my sweet, let us go and see this vicar of yours, I am sure he will be *very* understanding.'

Christopher was right. The Reverend Thomas Wainwright was most understanding and turned a blind eye to Christopher's address being the same as Laura's; he was used to young couples in this war and wanted to see them happy. He was pleased that they wished to marry in church and gave them his blessing. The wedding was fixed for 27 July, which was the day after Christopher returned from Salisbury Plain and two days before Laura was due to sail.

The two of them were happy for the rest of that day and Laura saw Christopher off at Paddington Station, then walked back to Peel Street in a maze of happiness and excitement.

Laura spent those three weeks in a

50

dream, partly of contentment and partly of apprehension. Christopher phoned her on two occasions and to hear his voice gave her some reassurance.

He arrived back at Peel Street in the evening before they were due to be married; he was happy and excited and he was also very fit after his weeks of training.

In the flat, he kissed Laura with great affection and held her in his arms for a long time. Laura felt her doubts slip away and was happy.

'Come and see what I've got,' he told her, and they went downstairs to find the smallest two-seater Laura had ever seen. 'She will get us out of London in no time,' he told her.

'Christopher, you haven't forgotten that we are to be married first, have you?' she asked him, a teasing note in her voice.

'I have not,' he declared, 'and tonight, I will sleep in your sister's bedroom very properly. I will make you mine tomorrow!'

'Oh, Christopher,' Laura sighed and knew happiness.

There were only five people at Laura's wedding, but she did not mind.

She and Christopher walked down Peel Street with a delighted Mrs Hancock, and were joined by a willing Mr and Mrs Dornford who had obligingly shut up the shop for half an hour so that they could be witnesses. Afterwards, they all went back to the shop, taking the vicar with them, to drink the couple's health with the best sherry available.

Back in Peel Street, Mrs Hancock waved them off in the small car and Laura and Christopher were soon out of London.

There was little traffic and they were on the A4 and through Slough in no time. In fact, they reached Maidenhead in time for a leisurely lunch and then made their way down the quiet roads to Marlow where they found their hotel on a secluded stretch of the Thames.

It was an old building and no more than a long, low sprawling cottage, built of red brick; it was set amongst trees, with the long lawns of the front garden running down to the river.

They were greeted by a cheerful proprietor who did not seem worried by ration cards and food shortages; his small establishment was very popular and in great demand by members of the forces on their short periods of leave.

'Mr and Mrs Leybourne,' he greeted them, and Laura smiled up at Christopher as she heard the words. We are very busy, but I have given you a small room overlooking the river. I hope you will be comfortable. We do the best we can when it comes to food and I hope to be able to give you a reasonable meal at six o'clock.'

He took them upstairs and when he had gone, Laura turned to Christopher and burst out laughing. 'He was expecting us!'

Christopher grinned. 'I phoned up and said we were just married. I wanted to be sure of a room; these small places near London are very busy. It was worth it, wasn't it?'

Laura looked round the room; low ceiling sloping under the roof and a tiny dormer window, dark oak furniture echoing the richness of the oak beams and the whole of the small room taken up by a large double bed. She went silent and Christopher encircled her with his arms.

'It's our little room, just for tonight, Laura. You really are my wife, aren't you? I haven't dreamed it all, have I?'

She had to laugh. 'Christopher, you are never serious. I just felt suddenly shy, as though I hardly knew you.'

'We've got the whole of the afternoon to talk to each other; you'll know me by the end of that time. Come on, let's go down to the river.'

It was nearly the end of July and although the sun was not shining, the cloud was high and light, and the air pleasant and warm. They made their way slowly through the garden and a little way along the river-bank, settling themselves under a willow at the water's edge.

Laura felt a sudden contentedness and any awkwardness seemed to drop away as they watched the gently lapping water and felt the green privacy of the trees around them. 'We couldn't have come to a more peaceful place,' she said. 'And the view down the river is lovely; I love to watch the water.' She turned and looked at him. 'I thought I would be frightened by water, but this seems a different world, doesn't it?'

He nodded. 'It *is* a different world. I don't think we could endure fighting and war if we couldn't find an oasis like this once in a while. It has to help store up strength for us to see us through the next conflict.'

Laura frowned. 'But, Christopher, there is no fighting in France now. Where are you likely to be sent next?'

He spoke solemnly for a moment. 'You musn't forget that Italy has declared war and we now have another enemy; the air force have already made raids on Turin and Milan. Fighting could flare up anywhere, we just have to be prepared.' He stopped and laid his hands on her shoulders. 'We also have to think that I may not be so lucky next time; there may not be a pretty nurse on hand to save my life.'

'Christopher, you can't joke about it . . .'

'I am not going to be serious today, Laura Terrington—no sorry, Laura Leybourne. That sounds nice, doesn't it?'

They talked the whole afternoon and did not move from their secluded hideaway under the trees.

Laura learned that Christopher had a brother who was in the air force and that they had been brought up in Yorkshire; but when she thought about it afterwards, she realized that he had said very little about his family and his home. She seemed to have done most of the talking, but she enjoyed the close companionship of the afternoon and it was with a light heart that she went back to the hotel to change her dress for dinner.

The meal was simple but good, and as the proprietor was able to produce a bottle of wine, it was a festive occasion.

In the fading light, after they had drunk their coffee, they walked once more along the riverside; the sky had cleared and the last rays of the sun were low down in the sky, reflecting a soft pink light in the water. The very stillness gave Laura a sense of uneasiness of the night to come. She knew she was being foolish, for she was no young girl; she had, however, lived a busy, sheltered life devoted to her nursing and the thought of the tiny bedroom with the large bed filled her with a fluttering nervousness rather than a joyous sense of expectation.

When they reached the room, she stood at the high small window catching a last glimpse of the shining water before she pulled the curtains.

She stiffened as she felt Christopher come up behind her; he linked his fingers round her small waist then raised his hands to fill them with the full roundness of her breasts. His fingers moved slowly and caressingly over the soft silk of her dress and she was suddenly overwhelmed by a surging throb of feeling and emotion.

His lips touched her neck and she heard him whisper. 'Are you a virgin, Laura?'

She was glad he couldn't see the flush on her face and she nodded her head and whispered quietly in return.

'Yes.'

'So am I.'

Laura did not know why his words surprised her, but the knowledge that it was a first time for him, too, filled her with a tender protectiveness; she turned in his arms and buried her face against him, glad to feel the soft stroking of his hand on her hair.

'I will undress you,' he murmured. His fingers reached for the buttons of her dress and she was thankful for his consideration and his light-hearted joking as he pulled the garment over her head.

When he joined her in the large bed and she felt the warm contact of his body, he was fully aroused and impatient. He was careful not to hurt her; then, just as Laura felt the first stirrings of her own response to his caresses, his climax came and he fell at her side crying out her name.

It's all over, Laura thought, and the tears came to her eyes. She had expected so much and she lay there beside Christopher, her body stiff and aching with an unfulfilled longing.

Perhaps it's always like that for a woman, she thought, but she knew she was deluding herself, and as she looked at her lover's sleeping face, she blamed her own nervousness and Christopher's inexperience.

She fell asleep quickly and opened her eyes just as it was getting light, with a momentary alarm at finding Christopher's naked body so close to hers. Then she felt him snuggle closer in his sleep and in the movement, knew the softness and the comforting warmth of his touch and his love. She nestled into him with a sudden desire of her own and his body instinctively responded and he was holding her close.

'Laura, my darling, darling girl, you are so beautiful, I want you all over again. It's barely light, but I don't need to see you. You do love me, say you love me, Laura.'

Laura knew she hesitated, but she could feel in herself the urgency of being one with him and she pressed closer. He took her wordless gesture as assent and made love to her again; Laura was happier that time. She experienced none of the wild joy she had expected, but was content to be one with this man who loved her so much.

They slept again and it was not until they were dressing to go downstairs for breakfast that Christopher was really fully awake and spoke with any sense.

They were partly dressed when he suddenly

57

sat her down on the bed and put his arms around her. 'Laura, you are more lovely than ever, you have made me so happy. Laura, I can't bear to part from you.'

'We have the whole of today together,' she told him. 'I don't need to be back in London until this evening.'

'What would you like to do?' he asked.

'It's my last day in England for a long time,' she replied. 'I think I would be happy just to stroll along the river with you; or I wonder if you can get a punt or a small boat on the river? That would be fun.'

They *did* manage to find a boat and Christopher rowed strongly while Laura sat lazy and smiling. She had not been sure that she loved Christopher enough to marry him, she was not sure that a rushed ceremony in the middle of a war was a good way of starting off a marriage to any man. But, she was thinking, if this feeling of contentment is love, then I am very lucky and very happy.

*　　*　　*

After their meal in the evening, they drove back to London, and in Laura's single bed at the flat, they made love and laughed together and were late getting up in the morning. Laura had her kit-bag ready, but in the end, it was a rush to get to the station and the goodbyes were said with laughter and tears amidst the noisy, steamy atmosphere, along with countless couples and families who were gathered round the doors and windows of the train with the same sad purpose of farewell.

CHAPTER THREE

Laura waved goodbye to Christopher from the train window, extricated herself from the four or five other people sharing the same small space and found herself a seat in a crowded compartment. She was the only female there and she did not see another woman during the whole journey, though her colleagues were there somewhere as she was to learn later. She sat squashed between two young sailors whom she soon discovered were from the ship she was joining, the *Queen Mary.* This fact formed an immediate bond and helped to pass the journey.

Not that Laura would have worried if she had no one to talk to for she had a lot to think about and half of her still seemed to be caught up in the whirl which had been the last two days with Christopher. It was almost as though she had been holding her breath for two days and had let Christopher Leybourne dictate the direction of her life.

She could not believe that she was married. Her identity card and papers still said Laura

Terrington—there had been no time to go to headquarters to change her name—but in her handbag was the slip of paper which was her marriage certificate. Christopher had insisted on her keeping it safe and, from time to time, she took it from her bag, saw their names and it seemed to be the only indication that she was, in fact, now Mrs Leybourne.

She decided then and there not to tell anyone and to keep her papers in the name of Terrington; it seemed the easiest way if she was going to be abroad for any length of time and unable to get things changed.

They tumbled out of the train at Southampton docks amid chaotic scenes, and not for the first time Laura was glad of the QAs' distinctive uniform; in a sea of khaki, it was very easy to pick out the few female figures in their grey and scarlet.

Then came an unexpected joy as she heard someone calling her name.

'Laura, Laura.'

She turned quickly and saw that it was Jenny Rowbridge and somehow they were hugging and crying at the same time.

'Oh, Laura,' Jenny said. 'I'm so pleased to see you, you've no idea. I lost sight of you in the crush at Dover and wondered if we'd ever meet up again. Were you on the train? I thought I was the only female on it!'

Laura couldn't stop laughing; it was so like Jenny and wonderful to think that they were going to be working together again. 'It's good to see you, too, and I was sure that I was the only nurse on the train; do you think we'll find some of the old crowd once we get ourselves organized? There must be a place where we're supposed to meet up.'

Their colonel came along not long after that and gradually the new unit was formed and they boarded the liner; there were many familiar faces and all of them glad to be back in action again.

They were a long time at sea and seemed to sail half-way round the world before they arrived in Greece, disembarking at Piraeus. They found rooms with a family in Athens for two nights while they waited for the instructions which would take them to their new hospital. But it was to be a frustrating time of waiting for them. They were placed in different hospitals in Athens for many weeks and made welcome by all the Greeks they met. Tensions were running high and it was not until November when Mussolini launched a treacherous attack across the Albanian frontier into Greece without any declaration of war, that they were moved. Many Greek families had young sons and husbands fighting in the mountains and casualties were pouring into the hospitals.

At last, they found out they were to be based in Kifissia, a lovely holiday resort in the mountains, where three of the hotels had been turned into a hospital. Jenny and Laura stuck together and were soon put to work in the largest of the hotels which took all the surgical cases.

It was there they were to meet their new MO, Dr Graham Neale.

Laura and Jenny and the other QA sisters had travelled from Athens to Kifissia in an ancient army truck; when they pulled up in front of a rather splendid hotel, with lovely views over sea and mountains, Laura jumped out first and hurried up to the imposing entrance. As she reached it, a man came out; a doctor—he was in his white coat with a stethoscope round his neck—and he looked bothered. She learned later that this was most unusual for him, but he, too, had just arrived and found problems.

He was not a tall man, not a lot taller than Laura, in fact, but he was of a strong build and had a head of thick brown hair, flecked with grey; his face was sympathetic and intelligent.

He walked towards her.

'Thank God you've come. Can you speak Greek?'

She must have looked at him as though she thought he was mad.

'No, I'm not mad,' he told her. 'I've only just arrived in Greece and don't know a word of the language, so I've got to find someone who can speak Greek. All the patients are either Greeks who have come down from the fighting in the mountains, or Albanian refugees who speak a little Greek. All the nurses and orderlies are Greek, and I can't find anyone who can speak English.'

She started to tell him how they had picked up basic Greek while working in the Athens hospitals, and she thought he was going to hug her.

'Thank goodness for that,' he beamed. 'I am Dr Graham Neale and I arrived from North Africa this morning. Are you the only sister they've sent?'

By this time, the others had joined them and he shook them all by the hand. 'It's very good to see you, but I must warn you that there's a lot of work to be done and some of the cases are difficult ones.'

They soon found him to be right; hastily they located their rooms and joined him on the wards. There were many cases who had been sent from the Casualty Clearing Stations and these were usually the most difficult to treat.

But after working all hours for a week, things began to change for the better. Refugees streamed in every day from Albania, many with frostbite, but as soon as they were treated, they were sent on to Athens, where temporary camps had been set up for them.

All the nursing staff got on well together and Laura soon discovered that Dr Neale was a very popular doctor. He was an older man, solid and serious, and when he started to seek out her company, she felt flattered. It was in no sense a romantic situation, but at the end of the day he seemed glad to have her to turn to for conversation; sometimes they put on their coats and walked in the garden of the hotel, enjoying the clear air and the sweet smell of the pine woods which ran down to the sea.

The talk was mainly about the day's work and rarely touched on personal things; Laura had no idea if he was a married man and had left a wife at home. She, herself, had no occasion to say anything about Christopher; it was a trust and a liking which developed between them and she found that she enjoyed it, for there was never any way in which she could feel she was being unfaithful to Christopher.

Jenny teased her about the friendship with the doctor and Laura thought at times that her friend seemed a little put out, though she had never neglected Jenny and the two were still very close.

So the winter passed. The Greek soldiers fought with considerable tactical skill in the mountains and drove the Italians out; but by the spring, the threat was coming from the other Axis power and on Sunday, 6 April 1941, Germany declared war on Greece.

Laura thought she would never forget the next ten days; the spirits of the Greek people were so low that they didn't seem to be the same nation the nurses had grown to know and like so well.

Life in the hospital was chaotic and they all worked harder than ever admitting convoy after convoy of the wounded with nowhere to put them; there were patients everywhere, many of them lying on blankets in the corridors.

The Germans were advancing and the day came when the news went round that they were only thirty miles away; only two days later, Jenny and Laura, who were working as a team on one of the acute wards, were told to be ready in half an hour as they were being evacuated. Greek nurses were coming in and Laura was told to give morphine to the patients who needed it most.

How Laura got all her stuff together in the time available she never knew; the sense of extreme urgency in front of the advancing Germans seemed to give her a clear enough mind to be able to act quickly. All the QA sisters gathered together in front of the hospital and were packed into lorries; it was then that Laura learned that they were leaving some of the doctors and orderlies behind and that Dr Neale was one of them. She was leaving without even saying goodbye; in such a way did war play havoc with human emotions, she thought.

Laura and Jenny clung together for it was a terrible drive, full of dangers from bombers; it took five hours to reach the coast. They tumbled out of the lorry not knowing where they were or what was going to happen, but they were determined not to be separated from one another. With a case in one hand and kit-bag in the other, they struggled over rocks on the shore into a little steam launch which took them to a waiting ship. Thankfully, they got on board and crowded together with troops and the wounded into small cabins; they discovered they were heading for Crete.

Laura had a sudden sense of *déjà vu* when the bombs started to fall, and Jenny clutched her arm; she knew that Laura was remembering Dunkirk and the Thames pleasure-boat.

'Laura, it can't happen twice; have courage.'

Laura turned and looked into Jenny's familiar face; Jenny was older than her by about ten years, she was short and plump with lovely fair curls, always good-tempered and able to see the bright side of things.

'Thank you, Jenny,' she said quietly.

The ship did not receive a hit and they arrived in the beautiful island of Crete, but in no mood to appreciate the bright sunshine and the sandy bays and hills.

They were taken to the General Hospital; it was crowded with wounded from the mainland and their help was desperately needed. But there was nowhere for them to sleep, and in the end they were taken to a cornfield where a camp had been set up; there was little to eat except bully beef and biscuits, but they had to make do and hurry back to the wards.

Jenny and Laura staggered off duty that night, both of them exhausted.

'I've never been so glad at the thought of a tent,' said Jenny, as they found their way in the dark.

There was a lot of unusual activity around the tents and Laura looked in amazement. 'Don't speak too soon,' she said, and started to laugh in a weak and silly way. All their stuff had been taken out of the tents which were filled with even more wounded. 'It's a good job that it's a fine night, I think we are going to be sleeping under the stars!'

They tried to get comfortable wrapped in blankets, and were nearly asleep when Matron came to tell them that they had to be ready to leave for North Africa by five o'clock the next morning. They did manage a few hours' sleep before getting up and groping around in the half-light before dawn, trying to get their possessions together. Laura found that she was past caring as they were herded into lorries like animals, taken to a small bay nearby and put on to an old Greek ship.

They were soon to find that setting sail was a pantomime; half the crew had deserted, frightened of the air-raids, but some of the troops on board offered to help, then there was another delay because the water supply had not been taken on, but at last they got off and on that first day, made good progress.

Jenny and Laura stayed on the deck; they preferred it to their cabin which was no bigger than a cupboard and smelled foul. It meant they were out in the open when the first of the air-raids came, but they put on their tin hats and decided to brave it; the ship was in convoy, which gave them some comfort.

Having Jenny as a companion helped Laura more than anything, and one day the conversation turned to Dr Neale. Laura did not know what had made Jenny pose her sudden question.

'Do you think that Dr Neale will get out of Greece, Laura?'

Jenny sounded very serious and Laura looked at her. We just don't know, Jenny, anything can happen. I can hardly bear to think that we shall never see him again. I've never forgotten losing Dr Kinghorn at Dunkirk.'

'Do you like Dr Neale, Laura?'

What an odd conversation, Laura thought, what is Jenny thinking of?

'Yes, I like him a lot, he is a fine man and a good doctor, too.'

'Did he tell you about his wife?'

Laura looked at Jenny again, but her face was giving nothing away. 'No,' she replied. 'I often wondered if he was married, I always thought he seemed like a family man, but he never mentioned having a wife. Why do you

68

ask?'

Jenny was silent for a moment. 'Matron told me about him one day. He had lost his temper over something, which was unusual for him, and when he had gone out of the room, she said "Poor man", and she told me.'

'Told you what?' Laura asked curiously and a little impatiently.

'It happened a few months before he came out to Greece. He and his wife and his two children lived in a village just outside Cambridge, it was on a busy main road. Mrs Neale had started to use her bicycle to get about because of the petrol rationing; one day when she was out shopping, she was hit by a lorry in an army convoy and she was killed. Wasn't that dreadful?'

Laura was silent, feeling waves of sympathy and sadness going out to the kind doctor. No wonder he had tried to lose himself in his work.

'I'm sorry.' It sounded inadequate. 'It explains why he has never spoken of his family. I wonder what happened to the children? It must be an awful worry for him, apart from losing his wife.'

Jenny knew that, too. 'They weren't tiny children, I think they were both in grammar school; after their mother died, Dr Neale's sister came to live with them. So at least he's still got his home together.'

'Well, I hope for their sakes that nothing

happens to him, too. I wonder if we will ever find out?'

'Probably not,' said Jenny, and once again changed the subject. 'Do you think we'll stay in North Africa?'

The conversation changed to a discussion of what they knew was happening in the war, gleaned from various sources and the occasional wireless broadcast. It was now the end of April 1941. Rommel and the German forces had landed in Tripoli in February and had fought their way as far as the Egyptian frontier; Tobruk had not fallen, but was besieged and there was a hospital there. This was one of the possibilities for any of the nurses.

The voyage lasted just one more day, and Laura felt that she had never been so glad to see the back of any ship as she was when they disembarked from that old Greek vessel at Alexandria.

All the sisters managed to keep together and found themselves being put on the first train for Cairo; they all felt tired and dirty, and arriving in a strange middle-eastern country seemed like being plunged into the unknown.

But all their doubts and miseries were more than compensated for by the welcome they received at the hospital of the Egyptian capital; the unit was expected and the matron made sure that they had a good meal, a hot bath and a proper bed to sleep in.

They did not stay in Cairo for many weeks, but long enough to re-equip and to get used to the climate.

Thinking about it afterwards, Laura came to the conclusion that she never did get used to it as she did not seem to be well the whole time she was in Egypt. She had never liked hot weather very much, and when they arrived it was in the middle of a heatwave, with a scorching wind blowing from the desert. The flies drove them all mad, and each one of the sisters went down with some sickness or other before they became adjusted to it.

When they were finally moved, there was a good and bad side to the arrangements. The unpleasant thing was that they were split up; some stayed in Cairo and some were sent to the general hospital in Alexandria. Laura and Jenny and two of the others found that they were the lucky ones, as they were sent further south to a desert hospital. Laura felt as though it saved her life to get out of the city.

On the morning they were to be moved, a truck came to pick them up and it was a long, bumpy journey along a poor track. When they reached El Nasa, it was to find that the hospital was still in the process of being built and the whole unit was in tents.

Laura decided straight away that she must have been brought up with a romantic idea of the desert, probably from reading her mother's copy of *The Sheik* by E.M. Hull when still a young girl and from seeing Rudolph Valentino in the film.

The romance lasted about two minutes while they stepped stiffly out of the truck and saw the partly constructed hospital and the tents where their temporary quarters were going to be. But she tried to look on the bright side and saw straight away that although the hospital was sited in typical desert conditions, it was near a lake and with a low range of hills to the west which sheltered the whole area from the worst of the winds coming across the desert.

When they were taken to their tents, they found that they had been given one each, but also that they were greeted by a film of sand over everything. Laura shook the blankets out and felt a dry constriction in her chest; by the time she had got the tent tidy and some of her essential possessions unpacked, everything was covered with sand again.

Laura never did get used to the sand; even when they moved out of the tents into the finished hospital, it was impossible to keep the sand out of the wards. They would tidy up in the morning, but in a few hours, sand was covering everything again. In the end, they became accustomed to it and began to enjoy it there.

They hadn't been in El Nasa for more than half an hour when Jenny and Laura received a lovely surprise. Their tents were next to each other and they were laughing at their futile attempts to get rid of the sand; by that time, they were feeling hungry and decided to go and look for the mess tent.

As they walked around, trying to sort out one large tent from another, Jenny suddenly cried out.

'Laura, look!'

There was such gladness in her voice that Laura glanced at her quickly; Jenny's face was glowing with pleasure and joy and she was pointing to a doctor talking to a group of nurses at the entrance of what proved to be the mess.

It was no wonder that Jenny looked so happy, for it was Dr Graham Neale; she started to run and Laura followed more slowly. But he had spotted them and broke away from the group and started to hurry towards them. When Laura reached him, Jenny was being hugged in delight and then he turned to Laura, his face lighting up. She, too, received a hug.

'Laura, Jenny.' He was as pleased as they were.

'We didn't know if you'd got out of Greece,' said Jenny.

He nodded. 'Yes, it was dicey, but I left as soon as I was relieved, two days after you had gone. It was only just in time and we had a nightmare crossing to Alexandria.' He was all smiles. 'It is lovely to see you. Where did you end up?'

Jenny told him how they had gone first to Crete and then about their stay in Cairo, and how thrilled they had been to be posted to a desert hospital.

He roared with laughter. 'Oh, you girls,' he said, and echoed Laura's own thoughts. 'You can forget about romance in the desert and concentrate on heat exhaustion and dysentery, not forgetting the sand . . .'

'We've already discovered the sand,' Laura interrupted. 'Is it always like this?'

'You haven't seen a sandstorm yet,' he laughed in reply, and they all started walking into the mess tent. 'It's not so bad at this time of year, but I'm told we'll know what's hit us when there's a really bad storm.'

They soon settled down to a new routine, and in a few weeks were thankful to be out of the tents and into the huts which had been built on the nearby site. Their patients were mainly prisoners of war, with many Italians amongst them; some of the officers spoke English and French, but they were very antagonistic towards all the English nurses.

Laura often thought what a strange thing it was being a nurse in wartime when your patients were prisoners of war. They were the enemy, but when a man is sick or injured, he becomes not one of the hated foe, but a human being who needs help.

It was during this time, if they had worked through the hot day, that Laura and Jenny took to taking a walk towards the lake in the evenings. They were just setting off one evening when Dr Neale came running to catch them up.

'Do you girls mind if I come with you?' he asked. 'I know you go down to the lake; it makes a change to be out of doors, doesn't it?'

Jenny stayed silent, suddenly and uncharacteristically shy, and it was Laura who spoke. 'It is nice to be out at this time of day,' she replied. 'And we are lucky to have the lake so near.'

And so the evening walks became quite a custom with them. Sometimes, if Laura and Jenny were on different duties, Laura would stroll with the doctor on her own, and as the weeks went by she came to value the quiet hours spent with him. He tried to get her to call him Graham, but she never remembered and it became a joke between them.

It was early in July that she began to feel unwell, sick and dizzy and generally out of sorts, finding it a struggle to get through her day's work.

In the evening, she was glad of the quiet walk to the lake and felt better for it; she put it all down to the heat. One evening when Jenny was not with them, Dr Neale stopped by the lakeside and Laura could feel that he was looking at her with some concern.

'You look pale, Laura, are you all right?' he asked her.

She looked across the water, the moon was rising and was reflected in the stillness of the lake, the sky was a deep blue and it was very quiet. Quite a romantic place, she was thinking, little knowing that there was romance in the air.

'Yes, thank you, I am all right now,' she told him. 'The heat seems to get me in the day, but these evenings are lovely.'

'You are lovely, too, Laura.'

There was a softness in his voice and she looked up sharply at his words. It was most unlike him to make any personal comment and she did not know how to take it.

So she laughed. 'I am getting old while the war is going on,' she said; but it was the wrong thing to say. She felt his hand on her arm as he turned her to face him.

'You are young and lovely, Laura, and I have come to care for you so much. No, don't look shocked. I have tried to keep my feelings to myself, but today I made up my mind to ask you to marry me.'

'Dr Neale . . .'

'No, please don't stop me, and please call me Graham. I long to hear my name on your lips. I have to tell you that I am a widower, my dear, and I have two growing children at home in England; but more than anything in the world, I would like you to be my wife and to ask you to become their mother.'

He was holding her hands by this time and

76

she was looking at him in bewilderment. She felt sick and dizzy as she had done earlier in the day, and didn't seem to know if it was the shock of his pronouncement or the total realization that she had forgotten about Christopher. She never thought of him. Days would go by and she was Sister Terrington; she had nothing to remind her and no feeling that she had ever been anything else.

But here was Dr Neale, kind Dr Neale, asking her to be his wife, and she was a wife already. A wife to Christopher.

She burst into tears.

There was a silence between them as the sobs came, and then she was in his arms and he was saying the same words over and over again.

'My dear girl, my dear girl.'

'Dr Neale . . .'

'Graham.'

'I can't, Dr Neale, I can't. I must tell you—'

'What must you tell me, my dear Laura? Are you going to say yes to me, did you understand what I was asking you? I want to marry you, Laura.'

She cried again.

'I can't marry you. It's so kind of you to ask me, but I can't marry you.'

'You don't love me, I am too old,' he said flatly.

Laura shook her head violently. 'No, it's not that, I am very fond of you. But you see, I have

77

never told anyone, I am married already.'

'You are married?'

'Yes.'

'Tell me.' That was all he said.

So she told him about Christopher and how it had all happened and she ended up in his arms again, sobbing afresh. 'But you see, I can hardly remember him, so much has happened. I keep forgetting about him, sometimes it seems that I'm not married at all. You are the first person I have told. Not even Jenny knows.'

She felt his fingers under her chin, tilting her face to look up at him, her eyes still wet with tears. Then he bent his head and kissed her, a long, loving and caring kiss, and she was left wishing that she could love him and be his wife.

He straightened up. 'Your Christopher can spare me one kiss,' he said. 'I hope that you will be very happy when you meet up again, Laura. This hasn't made any difference to our friendship, you needn't be afraid that I will make a nuisance of myself; we will still come down to the lake and watch the moon rise over the water. Sometimes you and me, sometimes the three of us.' He put an arm round her shoulders. 'Now I am going to take you back and we will go to the mess and I will get you a drink. I think you have got cold, my dear, you seem to be shivering.'

He was right. Laura was shivering and she

78

didn't know if it was from the emotion of the moment or because she really wasn't well.

When she reached the bedroom they shared, Jenny was already there, preparing to go to bed. She looked slightly put out, but Laura couldn't understand why until Jenny started to question her.

'Are you all right, Laura, you look flushed?' She was sitting on her bed, removing her stockings, and she did not look up when she said the next words. 'You didn't wait for me this evening, and you and Dr Neale were out for a long time. Am I to expect wedding bells soon?'

It was said with such an edge to her voice that Laura looked up sharply. It had hardly sounded like Jenny. She's jealous, Laura thought, Jenny's jealous. She's fallen in love with Dr Neale and she thinks I've stolen a march on her. Lots of little things Jenny had said came flooding back and she remembered the unaware expression she had often caught in Jenny's eyes.

Laura was feeling so wobbly, she could hardly face another emotional scene, but it was only fair to Jenny to tell her the truth.

'Dr Neale did ask me to marry him tonight,' Laura started to say, 'but I refused . . .'

Jenny went over and sat by her friend as though she could not believe what Laura was saying.

'You refused to marry Dr Neale? But,

Laura, he loves you. I know he is very fond of you at the least.'

Laura sighed. 'He may think he loves me at the moment, and I have a very high regard for him, but I cannot marry him. I cannot marry anyone; I am married already.'

Jenny stammered and could not speak. 'But, Laura . . .'

'It's true, Jenny, it happened before we sailed from Southampton and I didn't tell anyone, and since . . . well, since then it all seems so unreal and faraway that I can hardly believe that it really happened.'

'Do you want to tell me about it, Laura?'

Laura didn't really want to speak at all; her limbs were beginning to feel that they didn't belong to her, but she told Jenny briefly and the news was greeted with delight.

'I think it's wonderful,' Jenny said. 'And that means . . .'

'That means you can have Dr Neale all to yourself. You love him, don't you, Jenny?'

Jenny flushed and nodded. 'I can't help it, he's like the man of my dreams.' Then, in her usual fashion, she changed the subject and Laura found her friend looking at her closely. 'Laura, are you all right? You looked flushed when you came in and now you are shivering.'

'I haven't been feeling well all day and I started to shiver by the lake, but I thought it was the cool evening air. I'll get myself to bed.'

But suddenly, Jenny was all nurse and very

professional; before much time had passed, she had called the doctor on duty. Laura was dosed with one of the drugs that were used for some of the tropical diseases; then she was taken to the sick-bay and she knew she was ill.

For three days, she had a fever and didn't care whether she lived or died. She was vaguely aware of Jenny coming to see her, and on one occasion she thought she remembered Dr Neale holding her hand and taking her pulse. But those doctors in the desert had become expert on odd tropical maladies, and before a week was out Laura was sitting on the balcony of the ward, feeling better, but as weak as a baby.

Then the blow struck and it came from Dr Neale himself. They were sitting together in the shade of the balcony and Laura thought he looked stern.

'Laura, you probably won't like what I've done, but I've arranged to have you sent back to England and to be given a home posting for a while. I don't think this climate has suited you and you need a break from it. We'll drive you into Alexandria tomorrow in the truck and you will sail the next day. I shall send an orderly with you to make sure that you get on the ship safely.'

Laura listened to what he was saying in total silence, she didn't seem to have the strength to argue; he had got it all cut and dried so that she could make no protest.

Tears came to her eyes and she put out a hand to him. 'You are very kind and thoughtful and I won't make a fuss. I shall be sorry to go, but there is part of me that longs to see our green and pleasant land again.'

Laura thought he was relieved not to have to battle with her, and next morning he and Jenny were there to see her off; they stood together as they waved goodbye and Laura's final words came without her thinking of what she was saying.

'Goodbye. Take care of Jenny, Dr Neale.'

And her last sight of them was to see his arm going round Jenny's shoulder in a caring gesture which, to Laura, was full of hope and promise.

CHAPTER FOUR

Laura walked slowly down Peel Street. There was a damp drizzle in the humid air of late July which, combined with an acrid taint, came as a reminder that London was suffering from air-raids. From the bus, she had seen the shocking and sad evidence; wide gaps in what had been tidy rows of tall terraced houses, and burnt-out and shuttered shops. Even Mrs Dornford's shop had been closed, but it didn't look shut down; Laura decided to go straight to the flat and try the shop again later.

She had almost reached her own house when she stopped and looked at the other side of the road to stare in dismay and disbelief. She had escaped from Dunkirk, she had been evacuated from Greece, she had tended the prisoners in the desert, but nothing she had seen or done registered the futility of war so forcibly as the sight that met her *eyes* as she gazed at the space where three houses opposite the flat had been.

On the blank walls left exposed, she could see flowered bedroom wallpaper; the little black cast-iron Victorian grates showed their faces to the world, looking as though a maid had laid fires in them that very morning.

Tears blurred her eyes as she opened her own front door. France, Greece, Egypt; it had all been an ideological war in which she had felt she had been playing an intrinsic part. Here it was home, and it could so easily have been *her* home.

She stepped inside the house and as she reached Mrs Hancock's flat, the door opened and the little old lady stood there, frowning at first and then her face lighting up when she realized that it was Laura.

'Oh, Miss Laura, and me wondering who it was at this time of day.'

Laura gave her a hug and asked the halting question. 'Mrs Hancock, the houses opposite . . .'

'It's terrible, Miss Laura, two weeks ago it

was, and three of them killed. The others they dug out of the cellar and they were still alive, though badly injured; still in hospital they are, and the rest of us half-terrified when the siren goes. We've made our cellars into air-raid shelters, reinforced, too, and we've got benches and blankets down there; we can make tea, as well—someone brought us an old Primus stove. I shall have to show you. But now I'm going to make you a cup of tea and you can't say no. Where have you been and how long are you home for?'

Laura wanted to get up to the flat, but daren't offend the old lady and she learned that Mrs Dornford had just shut up for the day as she'd gone to see her daughter who'd had a baby. She was shown the cellar and promised that she would go down as soon as the siren sounded.

No, there hadn't been any letters for her, she was told, only the bills and those had been sent to Miss Dorothy.

Eventually, Laura climbed the stairs feeling weary. But the familiar, welcome comfort greeted her and she sank thankfully into her own chair.

She had been so certain that there would be news from Christopher—she desperately needed the reassurance of his very existence— but no, nothing. She was home, but she still felt the same void which she had felt in North Africa, the same emptiness and sense of not knowing what her feelings should be. The voyage home from Alexandria had not been without its hazards, for they had been in convoy and continually attacked from the air in the night; but the days were generally quiet and Laura had been able to sit peacefully on the deck, relaxing and enjoying the sunshine which had lost the fierceness of the desert heat. She had thought of Christopher because it had given her a shock when Dr Neale had asked her to marry him and she had realized how easily she had forgotten the man who had become her husband.

Now back in London, in her own flat, she sat for a long time, suddenly sapped of energy; she had so looked forward to coming home and now it seemed an anticlimax.

It was too late in the day to go to the Food Office, and her visit to headquarters would have to be made in the morning. In the meantime, she had to eat and decided that the easiest thing would be to walk into the West End and have a meal at a restaurant.

They were only disturbed for an hour that night. When Laura heard the siren, she put on a coat, picked up her gas-mask and joined Mrs Hancock at the foot of the stairs. The family from the second-floor flat were already in the cellar, and when Laura reached the dark and damp little room she was relieved to see that someone had lit a small oil-lamp so that they were not in complete darkness. There were no windows in the cellar so the light did not offend the blackout regulations.

Laura sat next to Mrs Hancock and she knew that her shivery state was not due to fear, but to the damp chill of the cellar; she had to hope that it wouldn't lead to a recurrence of her fever. She was glad of the cheerfulness of Mrs Hancock and the Cockney common sense of Mr and Mrs Briggs and their daughter, Thelma, who was Laura's age and fascinated to hear about the life of a QA.

Not that conversation was easy under the noise that was going on outside; minutes after the siren came the rhythmic throb of the German bombers and Laura thought the sound was enough to send fear into anyone's heart. Then the bombardment began: thunderous crashes in the distance punctuated by the staccato bursts from the English fighters and the flak from the anti-aircraft guns; each individual sound struck an initial nerve of fear until it all seemed to become a commentary to their thoughts and tensions and their efforts at conversation.

The all-clear is a lovely sound. It comes at least half an hour after the last of the planes has gone over, and during that time you have begun to feel safe again. The long steady blast of the siren reinforces the feeling of safety and survival; life can return to normal.

Laura slept well the rest of the night and awoke with a renewed vigour; the lethargy and despondency of the day before had gone, and she set off on her errands in good time.

At her headquarters, she was given a medical and pronounced fit; but, they said, it would be foolish to return to the climate of North Africa, and asked her if she would be willing to accept a London posting for a few months. Laura hadn't expected this, but didn't take long to make up her mind. She had the flat, and a spell back in England might give her the chance of meeting up with Christopher if he came home on leave. She agreed to this proposition, was given a week's leave and told to report to Woolwich barracks at the beginning of August.

Then she had to confess to her marriage, and she came out of the offices no longer Sister Terrington, but henceforth to be known as Sister Leybourne. On the way home, she had her identity card changed and got herself fixed up with a ration book and clothing coupons.

Back in the flat, she knew she would have to make up her mind what to do with her week off. She could visit Dorothy, she could go to Cumberland to see her parents, but what had been at the back of her mind was something completely different.

She was uneasy about Christopher and the lack of news. She felt that the only way of finding out would be to visit his home in Yorkshire; surely he would have written to his parents? She knew his address; it was Hayle House, Richmond, in the North Riding of Yorkshire.

Twenty-four hours later, she was in a train slowly pulling into Richmond station. It had not been an easy journey for the train had been packed with soldiers going to the garrison at Catterick; they all piled into the army lorries which were waiting for them.

Laura felt nervous and anxious; perhaps it had been silly to come unannounced, but it would have taken up too much time and too many explanations to have written first.

She asked for directions and was sent into the town to ask for Joe Sleightholme; he would take her out there, she was told. There were no taxis, the man at the station said, but Joe got a petrol allowance for taking people about. He wouldn't mind running her out there; been out there several times this last week he had, with all the goings on.

Laura was completely mystified. Why the constant reference to 'going out there'? Christopher had referred to his home in Richmond, but the man had made it sound as though Hayle House was outside the town. And what were the 'goings-on', as he had put it?

Feeling more nervous than ever, she found her way to Joe Sleightholme's house without any difficulty; there, she was greeted by a rather taciturn elderly man who said yes, he

88

would run her out there.

She got into the old Singer and they were out of the town in no time; she was told in few words that this was the back way to Marske. The name didn't mean anything to her, but she was thrilled by the view from her side of the car. They had left the old stone houses of Richmond behind and she found that she was looking over fields to distant woods and hills.

She was expecting to come to a village at any moment, and when the car turned in through tall pillars and drove slowly up a long drive with lime trees on either side, she began to feel uncomfortable.

Then the house appeared in front of her and her heart missed a beat.

It was the most beautifully proportioned Georgian mansion she had ever seen, built of the same stone she had seen in the streets of Richmond, mellow, soft and ageless, its three storeys of windows in perfect proportion and overlooking a circular, gravelled courtyard.

The house could only be described as gracious, set in a framework of tall trees with many smaller buildings to one side. Laura looked at it and realized that she had been brought to a country house of some importance. At its exact centre was an elegant porch, pillared and with steps leading up to an imposing and heavy door.

He must have brought me to the wrong place, Laura thought, as she looked across at

Joe Sleightholme. But he was already getting out of the car, holding open her door and saying in a gruff voice, 'Two shillin'.'

Laura searched for her purse and paid him, at the same time framing her nervous question.

'Is this Hayle House?'

'Always was, still is,' was all he said and he got back into the car, driving off and leaving Laura confronted with the flight of steps and solid oak door.

Christopher didn't tell me anything about himself, she remembered. I suppose his mother and father must be here; I'll just have to pluck up courage.

She climbed the steps and lifted her hand to the gleaming brass door knocker, letting it drop once to a sound which seemed to reverberate around the quiet court at the front of the house.

The door was opened and a small, plump woman in a flowered overall stood there. Laura couldn't find her voice. Was this Christopher's mother?

'Yes, miss?' the woman said in a not unfriendly voice.

'Mr Leybourne, is he in?' Her voice was the merest whisper.

'Do you mean Mr Nicholas or Mr Christopher?' The question was asked politely. 'Mr Christopher's not here.'

'No, not Christopher . . .' Laura felt even

more flustered. 'I wanted to see his mother or his father . . . if possible.'

The woman frowned. 'I don't know who you are, miss, but Mr Christopher's father died last week.'

Laura felt her mouth sag. What had she done? She felt like turning away, then she heard a voice from inside the house.

'Who is it, Mrs Maw?'

'A young lady who seems to know Mr Christopher.'

'My God, that's all we want.' Laura heard the edgy, irascible voice, the owner of which sounded not unlike Christopher. 'You'd better show her in.'

'Come in, Miss . . . ?'

'Miss Terrington.'

Laura didn't know why she said it; it was partly because she could never think of herself as Mrs Leybourne and partly because she was so completely bewildered by the situation in which she found herself.

The woman who seemed to be Mrs Maw held the door open for her and Laura climbed the steps, small case in one hand and the other nervously clutching her handbag. She heard the door being shut behind her and looked around. She was in a large entrance hall, completely square, laid with small but colourful rugs on a gleaming wooden floor; it was furnished quite sparsely with elegant chairs and a glass cabinet full of pieces of fine porcelain. What struck her most about the room was that each wall was lined with paintings and portraits; some of them were country scenes in sombre hues, others typical portraits of the eighteenth and nineteenth centuries.

These things she had seen in a flash, for confronting her was a very tall man. And not just tall, but broad-shouldered and heavy-limbed; at that moment, he was standing very stiffly in a black suit and black tie. His hair was dark, his eyes were dark, too; he was a very handsome man, but his good looks were marred by a frown which almost amounted to a scowl.

As he spoke, she heard the echo of Christopher's voice again and she looked at him carefully. His looks were so dark and his manner so disagreeable that she did not think it possible that he was Christopher's brother. Maybe a cousin, she thought.

He did not offer to shake hands and his voice was prickly with suspicion.

'Miss Terrington, I've no idea who you are or what you are doing here. You seem to have some acquaintance with Christopher.'

Laura met the brown eyes and felt dislike; not only for the superior expression, but also for the autocratic note in his voice. Who was he, she wondered? She did not move and felt a sudden defiance. It gave her the courage to speak.

'Christopher told me that he lived at Hayle House in Richmond, but he said nothing about his family.'

If possible, the stranger was even more starchy. 'You are obviously not well acquainted with him. Why are you here?'

Laura felt more nervous than ever. 'I was hoping for some news of him. He has not written to me and I thought his family might have heard from him.' She spoke clearly, but this man was still giving her the feeling that she had committed a great error in coming to the house.

'And what are you to Christopher that you were expecting news of him?'

The tone was arctic and had the effect of creating a surge of anger which swept through Laura and made her tell the truth.

'I am his wife.'

In the silence which followed, Laura felt as though the words were echoing through the hall; his wife, his wife.

'I beg your pardon?'

'I am Christopher's wife,' she repeated, and she was glad to hear the firmness in her voice.

'But you have just announced yourself as Miss Terrington.'

She faltered. 'Yes, I am sorry, it is very complicated. I have never been known as Mrs Leybourne and for the moment, I forgot.'

'Young woman, I believe you to be talking nonsense. You cannot be Christopher's wife, he would never have married without telling his family.' He looked hard at her; the brown eyes had no warmth.

Laura, for an awful moment, thought she was going to cry. She did not understand anything, only that this beast of a man who sounded like Christopher, but did not look like him, did not believe her. She did not trust herself to speak and she clutched at her handbag; in doing so, she remembered that her marriage certificate was in it.

With fumbling fingers, she undid the bag and found the piece of paper. She handed it to the man in front of her and spoke with a flare of temper in her voice.

'Read that if you don't believe me.'

He took it from her and his frown deepened as he read it; she heard him mutter under his breath.

'Laura Terrington, nurse; Christopher Leybourne, soldier; in the presence of . . .' He looked up and said aloud, 'It is Christopher's marriage certificate.' He put his hand to his eyes and suddenly looked old, though he must have been no more than thirty years of age.

'You'd better come in,' he said flatly. 'We seem to have some explaining to do.'

He turned, walked to a door at the side of the hall and opened it for her. She followed him and found herself in a spacious and lofty drawing-room; valuable and gleaming pieces of Regency furniture were mingled with worn and shabby chintz covers on the settees and chairs; there were more pictures in heavy frames. Large French windows opened on to a long sweep of lawn, and at the end of the lawn Laura could see shrubs and trees; beyond that was a small wood.

'Sit down.' It was a curt order and she sank into one the deep old armchairs; but he remained standing and seemed to tower over her. She felt completely dominated. He was still holding the certificate and waved it towards her as though the piece of paper could explain everything.

'I think you had better tell me about this piece of nonsense,' he said.

It was not like Laura to get angry, but she found this man, his manner and his looks, infuriating; she was in no mood to guard her tongue.

'You know my name, you know that I am Christopher's wife, you might at least have the decency to tell me who *you* are.' Her voice ended on a gasp, she thought she had gone too far.

'Are you telling me that you are married to my brother?'

'Your brother?' Her voice rose on the question, but looking at him, she could see the likeness.

'Yes, Christopher is my younger brother. Are you telling me that Christopher had the audacity to marry you and yet did not tell you that he had a brother, did not tell you anything about his family? What kind of marriage is that?'

Laura felt defeated; however was she going to explain to this unbearable man who said he was Christopher's brother? How weak her story would sound.

'Well?'

He obviously expected her to speak.

'I met Christopher last year,' she said feebly. 'I was about to be posted abroad and he begged me to marry him before I went; so I did marry him and we only had two nights together. I was sent to Greece and North Africa and have just come home on leave. I expected there to be some news of Christopher when I got back to my flat, but there was nothing. I didn't know what to do, I wasn't to know if he was still alive even. He had given me his address, so I thought the best thing to do would be to try and see his family and . . .'—she slowed down and her voice tailed off— '. . . and I am here.'

The man who was Christopher's brother had walked to the window and, with his back to her, was staring across the lawn to the end of the garden. Laura wished that she had never come; could she somehow make her excuses and slip away?

'I'm sorry, I should not have come. It was wrong of me to have bothered you. I will go.'

As she got up and moved towards the door,

he turned away from the window. His face looked tired, his voice held a sardonic tone.

'No, do not go. It seems I have lost a father and gained a sister-in-law all in one week.'

'You mean . . . ?' Her voice was hoarse.

'Yes, I mean that my father died last week and was buried yesterday . . .' He stopped. 'But then, if Christopher told you nothing, I suppose it must be my duty to tell you something of the family you have married into.'

Laura sat down in the chair again and looked at him; then he too sat down and, in her bewilderment, she gave a sigh of relief. He did not seem so menacing when he was seated.

'Christopher is my younger brother, there were just the two boys. My father was Robert Leybourne and my mother is Jocelyn, she is upstairs somewhere. My father was a lawyer, the head of an old firm of solicitors in Richmond, though he was not an active partner; Christopher and I are the junior partners. Father had inherited Hayle House and the Hayle estate, and it was his joy to run it on his own; it is a big estate, you see, with several farms.'

He paused and looked around him. 'You can see that Hayle House is old; it has been the home of the Leybournes since Georgian times. I was the heir, it all belongs to me now, but Marcia—she is my wife—and I have no children, so if anything happens to me, it all goes to Christopher or to Christopher's children.' Laura was holding her breath and he was glaring at her. 'Is that enough for you?' he asked.

She could not take in what he was saying, his words fluttered through her mind and hardly made sense. Why had Christopher not told her about the estate and that the Leybournes were obviously a wealthy family? Why had he been so secretive?

To her embarrassment, she found herself stammering.

'I didn't know about Hayle . . . I didn't . . . I mean, Christopher . . . he did say he had a brother in the RAF . . . but I don't know why he didn't tell me. All he said was that he was a solicitor in Richmond . . .' She broke off and looked directly into his dark eyes. 'I have no claim on you, I simply wanted to know if Christopher was safe.'

He was about to reply when they both heard the sound of the door being opened.

Laura looked round and saw a lady standing there; she stood in the doorway and did not advance into the room. She looked to be in her middle-fifties, had pretty grey hair and Laura noticed that she had the same blue eyes as Christopher; she was dressed in black and when she spoke, her voice was soft and apologetic.

'I'm sorry to interrupt, Nicholas, but Mrs Maw has told me that there is a young woman here enquiring after Christopher.'

Nicholas Leybourne got up and walked to the door, putting out a hand and then speaking quickly.

'Come in, Mother, I'm afraid I have a shock for you.' He led her to where Laura was now standing. 'This young woman says she is married to Christopher.'

'Married to Christopher?' The older lady was visibly shaken. 'But . . . ?'

'Exactly, Mother, but she has a marriage certificate to prove it. I had better make some introductions and then perhaps you would like to talk to her. I'm afraid I find it all rather improbable.' He turned to Laura. 'This is my mother, and you must realize that she is still suffering from the sudden death of my father. I would rather you did not upset her any more than you can help. Mother, this is the young woman who announced herself as Miss Terrington, but now says that she is Mrs Christopher Leybourne. Her name is Laura.'

Mrs Leybourne was the same height as Laura and looked at her seriously; she was composed, but there was still a shimmer of tears about her eyes, a slight shakiness in her posture. But her voice was clear and firm.

'Have you really married my Christopher?' she asked.

Laura nodded. 'Yes, Mrs Leybourne.'

The lady who was now Laura's mother-in-law gave the slightest of smiles. 'I can hardly take in what you have said.' Then she turned to her son. 'Nicholas, you can leave us on our own, I am sure you have a lot of things to see to. No, do not frown, I am quite all right and perhaps it will do me good to think of somebody other than Robert.'

He was about to make an objection, but changed his mind and helped his mother into a chair facing Laura; then he left the room without saying another word.

Laura felt as though she was drowning. She had expected to meet a Mr and Mrs Leybourne, older images of Christopher; instead she was faced with a suspicious brother-in-law and a recently widowed Mrs Leybourne.

They were both of them silent, summoning up their thoughts at this unexpected meeting; Laura saw a face with sad eyes, but full of an infinite sympathy. She saw the dignity of Mrs Leybourne, the courage of a mother with two sons fighting in the war and the human lost look of the recently bereaved. She had loved her husband, Laura thought, I must be kind to her.

What she hadn't been prepared for was outspokenness, friendliness and an immediate acceptance.

'My dear,' began the older woman, 'I have suffered one shock in this terrible week and you have just given me another one. Nicholas is cross with you, he doesn't want to believe what you say. But I believe you; if you say you have married Christopher and have the certificate then I have to believe it and I have to welcome you into the family. You have a quiet beauty and I can see the intelligence in your eyes, and I can see honesty and fearlessness. Christopher would have liked all of those things. I have a feeling I know why he did not tell us that he had married you, but I don't want to go into that now. I want to know about you yourself. I want to know all you can tell me about Christopher. We've had no word from him, you know, not since he was at Dunkirk. He was always very naughty about writing letters . . .' She stopped and looked at the young face in front of her. 'Why, what is it, Laura? I am going to call you Laura. What have I said to make you look like that?'

'It was when you said Dunkirk. You see, that was how we met; Christopher saved my life . . .'

Mrs Leybourne was staring now. 'But, my dearest girl, we had a phone call from Christopher after Dunkirk. He was in a hospital in Dover; it was a terrible line. He was all right, he said, just a crushed foot and he'd got out of France safely and a young nurse had saved his life at Dunkirk, then the line went dead. He was speaking to his father, I didn't even get a chance to talk to him.' She leaned forward and touched Laura's hand, the first encouraging gesture Laura had received since

101

entering Hayle House. 'I think you'd better tell me everything.'

Laura drew a deep breath. 'I am a nursing sister in the QAs and I met Christopher on an ambulance train coming out of France; eventually we got to Dunkirk and we were taken off in an old Thames pleasure-boat. I was with him on the deck when we were hit by a bomb—I am sorry, it is still hard to think of it for it was dreadful—the boat was in flames and we had to jump into the sea. I managed to get Christopher over the rail and pushed him into the sea, and then I jumped, too. He was a good swimmer and we were making for a raft which had been put out by a destroyer . . . I thought I was going under, but he held me up, he saved my life.'

'And you saved his.'

Laura nodded. 'Not many from the pleasure-boat got away and it blew up very soon afterwards.'

Neither of them spoke for a while, Laura inwardly trembling at the retelling of those horrifying moments, her mother-in-law going over the story in her mind and thinking of her next question.

'And you stuck together after that?'

'No, not exactly. I left him at the hospital in Dover and went back to London. Christopher was sent to a hospital in Barmouth in North Wales though I didn't know that till afterwards. About three weeks later, he sought me out at my flat in London.'

'And then?'

Laura smiled. 'He asked me to marry him, but he was being sent off to Salisbury Plain to recuperate, so we had the banns called and were married when he returned. We had two nights together in a hotel at Marlow, on the Thames, but I had to report for duty the next evening and it was the last time we saw each other. I have been in North Africa and when I came home there was no word from Christopher. You know the rest. Sometimes I wonder if I really did marry him and have to look at the certificate.' She looked straight into the eyes of Christopher's mother. 'I'm afraid your elder son didn't believe me.'

'I believe you, my dear Laura, and I think you should have a reward for bravery—'

Laura interrupted hastily. 'Oh no, it wasn't brave, it was just common sense, the kind of thing we are trained to do.'

'You risk your lives for your patients?'

'We are all risking our lives in this war, Mrs Leybourne, every minute, every second of the day and night.'

'You are a dear, brave girl and I am going to love you no matter what Nicholas thinks. He's had a bad week, called suddenly from his squadron when his father died, and the funeral yesterday and so many things to see to. It's not been easy for him.' She got up and started to walk towards the door. 'Now I am going to get us some tea and tell Mrs Maw—she is my housekeeper and cook—to prepare a room for you. I hope you will be able to stay with us for a little while.'

'I have to report to the Woolwich hospital next Monday, but I would like to stay for a night or two, if you are sure your son won't mind.'

Mrs Leybourne reassured her and went out of the room.

Laura sank back in her chair for a second as the waves of kindness from Mrs Leybourne seemed to wash over her. She was believed and she had met Christopher's mother; Christopher himself was no nearer, but she was in his home. She smiled for the first time; perhaps it would all work out happily after all, she told herself.

As Mrs Maw opened the door with the tea-tray, Laura could hear the sound of strident voices in argument coming from the direction of the hall.

'She is, I tell you, Marcia. I have seen the marriage certificate.'

'I don't believe it, I just don't believe it. Christopher would never have done such a thing.'

'Well, come and meet her, then. Mother has been talking to her . . . Oh, there you are, Mother, are we having some tea?'

'Yes, Nicholas. Marcia, I want you to come and meet Laura.'

'Jocelyn, I cannot meet anyone looking like this; I must go and change.'

But Mrs Leybourne had beckoned to Laura. who rose reluctantly from her chair and walked to the door.

In the hall, she met a haughty stare from a woman who was about as tall as Nicholas and was dressed in muddy corduroy trousers and a red shirt.

'Laura, I want you to meet Marcia, she is Nicholas's wife; Marcia, this is Laura, who has married Christopher. She has told me all about it and it turns out that she is the nurse who saved Christopher's life at Dunkirk.'

Laura, uncomfortable and embarrassed at being introduced in such a way, held out her hand to the new arrival, and it was taken briefly.

'I cannot believe that Christopher would marry without telling the family,' Marcia said, and Laura wondered how many more times she was going to hear these words. 'But I'm pleased to meet you, and I'll go and get bathed and changed and then come down for tea.'

She disappeared up a gracious curving staircase, and while Mrs Leybourne went back into the kitchen for another cup and saucer, Nicholas took Laura back into the drawing-room. His expression was no more agreeable than it had been an hour ago.

'My wife helps on a neighbouring farm as her part of the war effort,' he said, and added, in what seemed a rather derogatory way, 'she seems to enjoy it, and it keeps her occupied while I am away.'

Laura couldn't find a reply and stood awkwardly by the window; he joined her there.

'You seem to have ingratiated yourself with Mother. Is it true about you saving Christopher's life?'

Surely I haven't got to go through it all again, she asked herself, but Nicholas did not wait for a reply. 'When he phoned after Dunkirk, Father said he mentioned something about a nurse. Was that you?'

'Yes, it was.'

'Hell, I suppose it *is* all true then and I owe you an apology. I still can't believe it.'

Laura found that her tone was quite sharp. 'It's all been a lot for me, too.'

He looked at her as though seeing her for the first time. 'Yes, I suppose it was a shock coming here; it's hard to imagine getting married to someone you know nothing about. I've known Marcia all my life.'

'It happens a lot in wartime.' She spoke slowly and tried to form her next question carefully. 'Is it true that you've heard nothing from Christopher since Dunkirk? All that time?'

'That's right, not a word from him; we've no idea where he is and Mother has been quite upset, though she should know him if anyone does.'

106

Laura was thoughtful. 'His foot was a lot better, he was expecting to be back on active service at any time. I wonder where he was posted. If anything had happened to him, you would have heard officially, wouldn't you?'

'I presume so,' he replied. 'We've just got to assume he's a lousy correspondent, though it does surprise me that he hasn't even written to *you*. He'll probably turn up on leave one of these days, he always was a casual blighter.'

'Was he?' she said, without thinking.

He looked at her keenly and with some malevolence. 'You don't know him, do you? You know nothing about him; you married someone you didn't know. What kind of marriage is that?'

It was the second time he had asked her that question and Laura felt that she hated him. 'It seemed the right thing at the time,' was all the reply she could make, and she was saved from saying anything further by the arrival of his mother.

'Laura, I've been thinking about it. Marcia calls me by my own name, Jocelyn, and I rather like it, for it makes me feel younger. Would you like to do the same?' Mrs Leybourne smiled as she looked at Laura. 'No, poor girl, I'm rushing you, aren't I? Take your time and it will come. I expect Nicholas has been putting you through it, too; I hope that the two of you are not quarrelling. Come and have some tea and tell us something about yourself.'

Marcia appeared, dressed in a striking silk dress of a turquoise and white floral design which made Laura feel very shabby and insignificant in her printed cotton, no longer fresh after her long journey. She felt she was in for an inquisition, up for approval by the Leybourne family. Marcia was superior, Nicholas still disapproving, only Mrs Leybourne showed any kindness and understanding and Laura began to see in her the same lovable qualities she had found in Christopher.

Dinner that evening was not so awesome as Laura had feared and after the meal, when Nicholas asked her to walk with him in the garden, she was somewhat taken aback, surprised that he was seeking out her company. But having seen the long lawns and the small wood from the window, it all looked cool and inviting and it rather pleased her that she might have a walk and enjoy the evening air.

It was still mild and she did not need a cardigan; she walked silently at Nicholas's side down the path which appeared to lead directly into the wood.

She did not feel relaxed in his company and wondered at his purpose in bringing her out; she felt awkward in the silence, and in the end she asked him something which had been bothering her ever since her arrival.

'I would like to ask you something, Mr Leybourne.'

'For heaven's sake, call me Nicholas; it looks as though I am going to be your brother-in-law, doesn't it?' His tone was as irritable as it had been in the afternoon, but Laura persisted.

'When I arrived, why were you so certain that Christopher had not married me? You just wouldn't believe me, would you? And Marcia was the same.'

He glanced down at her, his look reflective, but still aggressive.

'I've brought you out here this evening to let you know why we all felt as we did and to tell you what the state of affairs is here at Hayle.' His voice became sharp. 'I did not believe you for the simple reason that when Christopher last left here to go off to France, he became engaged to the daughter of our nearest neighbour, Sir Anthony Coupland. Christopher announced his engagement to Meg and they planned to marry on his first leave. Everyone was very happy about it.'

CHAPTER FIVE

Laura felt as though Nicholas had hit her and she must have looked shocked.

He took her arm, but not roughly. 'I'm sorry

to put it so bluntly, but they were so happy. Now perhaps you can understand why I would not believe you.'

He was leading her along a grassy path through the trees until Laura found herself standing in the open and looking across the valley of the Swale. She almost gasped as the trees disappeared in a steep drop and she realized that she was standing on the edge of a cliff. Then she heard Nicholas's voice beside her.

'Yes, it is steep, isn't it? It is called Whitcliff Scar and the view is spectacular; we have put a seat here, come and sit down.'

Laura was thankful to be seated; her mind was racing with what Nicholas had told her about Christopher. 'I'm sorry,' she said falteringly, 'I was not to know that he was already engaged to be married. Christopher didn't say anything, it must have been why he was so secretive. But this Meg, what shall I do?'

Her companion spoke abruptly. 'I shall have to see her. I'll go over early in the morning before she starts work. She's on the farm, too, with Marcia, they are great friends. That's why Marcia wouldn't believe about your marriage either.'

'I'm sorry,' Laura said again. 'I'd no wish to break up a romance, but Christopher was so insistent, he wouldn't wait.'

'It sounds like Christopher,' Nicholas said

curtly, and Laura looked at him curiously.

The brothers were not at all alike; it sounded almost as though they had not been very close either, but Nicholas was looking very serious and when he spoke, his words came with a sudden rush.

'Look, Laura, I'm sorry you had such a bad reception when you arrived. It's not like me to be as bad-tempered as that, but I'm afraid that you seemed like the last straw. I've had the hell of a week; I'd been in the air for six nights on the run when I got the message about Father. I had to leave the men and come straight up; it all happened so suddenly, for Father was fit and well one minute and gone the next: he was only sixty. Mother broke down, but has made a wonderful recovery; she's got guts, you know, and somehow today it has helped her a lot to have someone to talk to. She took to you straight away, didn't she?'

'She is a darling,' Laura said simply.

'She has never got on very well with Marcia. I think it was a mistake sharing the house when we got married, but it seemed a sensible thing to do with me being in the RAF and Christopher away, too.' He gave an unexpected grin. 'Christopher has always been her favourite, the blue-eyed younger son; she has been very cut up because we've had no word from him. I think your arrival is helping her a lot, but she is going to be upset about Meg . . .' He stopped speaking and seemed lost in thought. 'I don't know, it seems such a mess!'

'Has Meg always lived near you?' asked Laura tentatively.

He nodded. 'We were all brought up together. Marcia's parents used to farm nearby before they retired and went to live in Richmond; Meg and her sister Lucy lived at Clapgate Lodge along the Marske road, and then there were Christopher and me. It seemed only natural that Christopher and Meg should want to get married; she is going to be heartbroken.' He turned to look at her and some of the careworn tiredness in his face was replaced by a practical look of kindly purpose. He smiled and she felt that she was looking at a different person; his eyes lit up, his mouth relaxed from its former stern and rigid lines, and she suddenly realized that he was a very good-looking man and not as old as she had first thought.

'I'd better tell you something about the family—typical of Christopher not to say a word.'

'He told me he was a solicitor.'

'Oh, he did get as far as that, did he? It is the family business in Richmond. Father may have owned the estate, but he wasn't wealthy and the farms and the grouse moor hardly supported the family, let alone kept Hayle House in order. One of his uncles started the law firm over a hundred years ago, and both

Christopher and I read for the law and went into the firm. But all that will change now; when this bloody war is over, I shall have the estate to manage and we'll get another partner for the firm.'

Laura felt that she had to say something. 'Hayle House is beautiful, isn't it?'

He gave a sudden grin. 'It may look beautiful, but it costs a fortune to keep it going and heating it is a nightmare. You are here in high summer! You've got to be tough to survive a winter at Hayle; we are right on the top of the cliff and seem to catch the worst of the snow and the winds. But I love it for all that, and now I won't have to find a home for Marcia and myself; we can bring up our family at Hayle, if she will agree to have a family, that is.'

The last words were said on a bitter note and Laura thought it strange that he should have said such a thing in front of her, but she made no comment. He got up and walked to the edge of the trees; he stood staring for a long time and then turned back to her. 'What a day, what a week,' he said soberly, 'but it is always good to come to this spot.' He looked at her keenly, but not critically. 'Laura, we got off to a bad start, and I apologize and hope we shall deal better in the future. I can't blame you for Meg being let down, it's that scapegrace brother of mine. But I mustn't say that, for presumably, if you are married to

113

him, you must love him. Shall we shake hands on it?'

She put her hand into his and found the strong coolness of his grasp very welcome and very reassuring, just as his words had been.

They walked back to the house to be met by Marcia hurrying over the lawn to meet them. 'Where have you been?' she asked petulantly. 'I've been looking for you everywhere.'

'I'm sorry, Marcia, but you knew I had to explain to Laura about Meg and Christopher.'

'I hope she's suitably repentant,' said Marcia, without even looking at Laura. 'I can't imagine how poor Meg is going to take it.'

Laura stood uncomfortably between the two of them, wishing that she could walk back to the house and leave them; but Nicholas was including her in the conversation and she listened to their slight argument.

'Laura is not to blame,' Nicholas said, and his wife looked at him sharply. 'Christopher has behaved very badly towards Meg and I shall have to see her to try and explain. I would rather you said nothing to her about it, Marcia, not until I have spoken to her at any rate. I'll go to the lodge first thing in the morning before she leaves for the farm.'

'You'll have to be up early then,' retorted Marcia, and her tone made Laura wonder at the seeming lack of sympathy between the two of them, but perhaps it could be explained by the difficult days of the past week.

114

They all returned to the house, and a little later Laura said goodnight and went up to the pretty bedroom she had been given; she didn't even try and get into bed, she thought she would never sleep. It was not yet dark and it was very warm; there seemed to be no air in the old house and she remembered the time spent with Nicholas under the trees with gratitude.

It seemed hard to think of him as Christopher's brother, and after her conversation with him she was left with an unsure sense of dismay at how little she had known of her husband before rushing into a marriage with him. And now I don't even know where he is, she said to herself; coming to his home had not solved *that* problem.

She thought with some pleasure of the kindness of Mrs Leybourne and looked forward to getting to know her better on the following day. Of Marcia, she was not so sure; there had been hostility in her attitude and the relationship between Nicholas and his wife seemed far from loving.

Laura also thought about Meg, the girl who believed that Christopher was going to marry her; she dreaded meeting Meg, it would be very hard to explain that Christopher had never made mention of the girl he had been engaged to.

She sat on the low wide seat at the window and pondered her dilemma, at the same time realizing that she would gain nothing by worrying. She gazed across the garden to the distant hills of Wensleydale; it all seemed so solid and permanent, all the things which war was not. The peaceful greenness of grass and trees helped her to relax until, at last, she undressed, got into bed and slept soundly.

Laura spent two days at Hayle. She quickly learned to love the old house, and on her walks down nearby lanes she learned to value the usefulness of the land which had served the family for centuries. I would like to live here, she reflected.

On her first morning, she went downstairs to breakfast to find the dining-room empty although she could hear voices from the direction of the kitchen. She opened the door to find her mother-in-law sitting at a large kitchen table drinking tea with Mrs Maw.

Mrs Leybourne turned to greet her. 'Laura, my dear, we always breakfast in here. Marcia was off to the farm early and Nicholas has walked over to the lodge to see Meg.'

Laura sat on a chair beside her, and Mrs Maw poured the tea and offered toast. But Laura could not eat until she had spoken 'Mrs . . . Jocelyn, I am very sorry about Meg, but I had no idea, you see.'

'Now stop worrying and eat some breakfast. Mrs Maw and I have been talking about it—she is like one of the family, you know, she has been with us since the boys were born—and

116

from something she has said, I think that things might turn out better than you imagine. I'm not saying more than that, for I know that Meg has always been very fond of Christopher and she was very excited when they got engaged.'

Laura felt a little reassured at these words, but she knew she would be glad when Nicholas returned and she had learned what he had to say.

After breakfast, she was shown over the whole house by Mrs Maw and found that it was not as rambling as she had supposed. Nicholas and Marcia lived in a self-contained flat which took up the whole of the third floor, with low sprawling attic rooms which were homely and appealing.

As Laura came down the main staircase into the hall, she saw her mother-in-law talking to a young woman by the front door. Laura paused and watched warily; the newcomer was short with a round, pretty face and loose brown curls cut short over her head. As she spoke, she seemed excited about something, and Laura, who had at first thought that it must be Meg, began to think that she was mistaken. She had expected to meet a Meg who was weepy and upset.

At that moment, Mrs Leybourne turned and spotted Laura as she descended the last few stairs. She smiled briefly and held out a hand.

'There you are, Laura; I want you to come

and meet Meg. She has come especially to see you and seems to want to speak to you urgently.'

Laura walked slowly across the hall, gazing at Meg in fascination as she took in the incongruity of the pretty brown curls and large blue eyes with the sturdy cords and khaki shirt the girl was wearing. She had no idea what she was going to say, she felt awkward and apologetic.

'This is Meg Coupland,' Mrs Leybourne was saying as the two shook hands. 'Meg, this is Laura who arrived so unexpectedly yesterday. You will have a lot to say to each other, so I will leave you.'

Although Laura felt embarrassed, she could not feel threatened by Meg: the girl in front of her was showing no signs of anger or the upset of tears which Laura's presence should have given her. Laura sensed that the interview was not going to be as difficult as she had imagined. 'I'm pleased to meet you, Meg, I'm afraid I've given you a bit of a shock. Marcia and Nicholas are furious with me; they wouldn't even believe me at first.'

Meg smiled. 'Shall we go out into the garden?' she said brightly. 'I'm not really fit to be seen indoors in these clothes; I was just setting off for the farm when Nicholas appeared. So I worked just for a couple of hours and then came straight here.'

Feeling perplexed at Meg's friendly attitude,

118

Laura followed her through the front door and around to the side of the house where there was a stone bench set back privately amongst overgrown laurels and golden privet.

'We always used to come here when we had something serious to discuss,' said Meg. 'No one can see us from the house or garden.'

Laura was glad that they were sitting out of the sun; what she had to say was not going to be easy and the green shade stopped her from getting hot and flustered.

'Meg,' she began, 'I know how shaken you must be by what Nicholas has told you, but you see I had no idea. It all happened so quickly and Christopher told me very little about himself; he certainly said nothing about being engaged already. I am very, very sorry, I don't quite know what to say.' Laura felt her lame excuses to be so inadequate and looked around quickly when she heard Meg give a laugh.

Then she felt the girl put a hand on her arm and she turned and met blue eyes which had a happy expression in them.

'Laura, you've saved my life,' Meg was saying. 'Please don't apologize; I've known Chris all my life and can just imagine him acting so impulsively. It was the same when we got engaged; you see, the family had always imagined that we would marry one day, and when Chris went off to France in such a rush, he begged me to become engaged before he

119

went. So I said yes to please him.'

Laura frowned, trying to understand. 'You mean . . . ?'

'What I am trying to tell you is that while I am very fond of Chris, I didn't truly love him; at least, not in the same way that I now know love to mean.'

'But, Meg . . .'

Meg would not allow the interruption. 'No, listen to what I have to tell you and then you will understand. You see, not long after Chris had gone, Nicholas came home on leave and brought a fellow RAF officer with him, Rob Campbell. His home is in Scotland, and Rob couldn't get there and back in such a short time, so Nicholas invited him here. I met him the next day.' She looked at Laura seriously. 'I fell for him, Laura, I completely forgot about Chris; Rob felt the same, we knew we were in love and it was like nothing I had ever felt before. Is that how you felt about Chris?'

Laura felt a sense of shock at Meg's question, for she had never been sure of the strength of her feelings for Christopher, she just felt very fond of him. She had certainly never felt the strong flash of feeling which Meg had just described, even when she had first met him in the train. It was difficult to reply honestly.

But she found that Meg was not waiting for an answer. 'Rob wanted us to get engaged, so of course I had to tell him about Chris. I

120

wouldn't have let him down, you know, not when he was away fighting. Rob wanted us to get married the next time he had leave, and I just didn't know what to say; I did want to marry him, but I kept thinking of Chris all the time. So you see, don't you, Laura, why I said you'd saved my life? You are married to Chris, so I am free to marry Rob. I could hug you, I really could!'

They both laughed then and Laura could feel only happiness for Meg, but there was one thing which still puzzled her and she asked the question directly.

'But, Meg, didn't you tell anyone, not even Marcia? I thought she was your friend.'

Meg shook her head. 'Not a soul; I didn't want to let them down. They think so much of Chris and were feeling badly enough, in any case, because they hadn't heard from him.'

Laura looked at the animated girl by her side. 'Didn't Christopher write to you either, Meg?'

'Not a word, I didn't expect him to. He was always hopeless at letters, relied on the telephone for everything. But his mother was upset and I felt sorry for her, and now Mr Leybourne has died; it's been a terrible week, what with not hearing anything from Chris, and Marcia and Nicholas quarrelling . . . Oh, I'm sorry, I shouldn't have said anything, but I've a feeling everything is not well in that quarter. You may have noticed yourself.'

Laura hardly knew what to say. 'I've only been here a day, but there were one or two things which made me wonder. I put it down to Mr Leybourne's death and the funeral.'

'No, it's more than that,' Meg said slowly. 'I shouldn't be saying it, for Marcia is my friend, but she doesn't seem to want a family and I think Nicholas is upset about it.' She stopped suddenly. 'I'm sorry, it's wrong of me to speak of them like this, but they worry me. But enough of them; I've taken a liking to you, Laura, and I hope that you and Chris will be very happy.'

'Thank you,' Laura replied. 'I think we would all be easier in our minds if we had some word from him, but it's just one of the fortunes of war, I suppose.'

Meg wanted to hear all about Laura's experiences as a QA, and they stayed on that seat until the sun rose high in the sky and crept through the leaves and branches of the shrubs and trees. Laura realized that Meg was a chatterbox, but she liked the girl enormously and was amused that she was the only one who shortened Christopher's name to Chris.

Laura left Hayle the next day, but before she left she was to have an argument with Marcia and another talk with Nicholas on his own.

It happened that when Laura went down to breakfast that morning, it was Marcia she was to find at the large kitchen table. She was

122

dressed in her usual working-clothes and Laura had the feeling that cords and shirts suited her better than the silks she wore in the evenings.

Marcia didn't even say 'good morning', but instead launched into a belligerent attack on Laura.

'I suppose you think that you and Christopher will be coming to live at Hayle now?'

Laura was taken aback and found it difficult to make a reply. She was cross with herself for stammering, 'I don't know . . . I don't think . . . Christopher didn't say . . . we didn't talk about where we were going to live. We weren't thinking about the future at all, you don't in the war somehow.'

Marcia grunted. 'Hmm, that's as may be, but I might as well tell you that you won't be welcome. It's bad enough sharing the house already.'

Laura was shocked; it sounded as though Marcia wanted Hayle House for herself, but where would Mrs Leybourne go?

'I am sure that Christopher will have his own ideas about where he wants to live,' she replied, and thought she sounded prim. 'He may prefer to be in Richmond if that is where the office is.'

'Well, I think you'd do well to encourage him along those lines; he and Nicholas would never manage to live in the same house. You realize that they are very different, I suppose?'

Laura felt miserable; here she was, hardly knowing Christopher, disliking his older brother and now having an altercation with her sister-in-law.

'It seems so unreal,' she was forced to say. 'I just wish that Christopher would get leave, or even that we knew where he was, then I might be able to give you some reply.'

Marcia looked at her sceptically. 'I believe you rushed into marriage knowing nothing of the man who is your husband.' Then seeing the look on Laura's face, Marcia stopped abruptly; realizing that she had gone too far, she amended her tone. 'But Christopher's a good sort, easy-going, not like Nicholas. I think you'll get on all right.'

With those words, she got up from the table and made her way out of the house without even saying goodbye.

Laura did not sit there for very long harbouring resentful feelings towards Marcia, for her mother-in-law joined her and they had a cheerful breakfast together. Laura was informed that Joe Sleightholme would come for her at eleven o'clock to take her into Richmond.

Then, for a moment, Jocelyn suddenly looked sad. 'I am going to miss you, Laura. I know that you came on the scene only a couple of days ago, but I had been dreading those days, and already you seem like one of the family. Somehow you seem to bring Christopher that much nearer.'

Laura tried to be cheerful. 'You've been very kind to me, Jocelyn, and I promise I will write to you.'

'Thank you, my dear, and I hope you will come up and see us whenever you get some leave, though I know you have your own parents to consider. But you will always be welcome. Life isn't going to be easy, I don't even know what is going to happen about the house. It belongs to Nicholas now, but maybe he will let me have the flat.' She stopped as she caught the expression on Laura's face. 'Marcia's been talking to you, hasn't she? I know she doesn't want me here, but I couldn't bear to leave Hayle, not yet at any rate. I suppose I will have to talk it over with Nicholas.'

Laura put out a hand; she felt unbearably sorry for the woman who had just lost a beloved husband and felt so insecure in the house she had known for so many years. 'Nicholas will want to know that you are safely here when he is away; after all, who would run the house with Marcia out all day?'

She knew she had said the right thing when she saw Jocelyn's smile.

'Thank you, Laura, I am sure you are quite right and I shall be too busy to mope. You never know, they might send us some evacuee children from London, though I suppose we are too much off the beaten track. Marcia would be glad to leave it all to me and Mrs Maw, for she loves her work on the farm and I know she wouldn't want to give it up to spend her time running a house. Now, you are not to listen to an old lady's fretting; you go off and pack your case and we will have time for coffee before you go.'

Laura bent and gave her a kiss and was rewarded with a brilliant smile as she made her way upstairs.

As she packed her small case, Laura wondered if she would see Nicholas again before she left and was surprised to hear a tap at the door. She found him standing there.

'Have you got time for a turn round the garden before you leave, Laura?'

'Well, yes, thank you,' she said with some hesitation, wondering why he should want to speak to her.

Outside, she felt small beside him and walked silently as he seemed to make his way to the wood at the end of the garden almost automatically.

They sat side by side on the seat looking over the dale, Laura thinking that it was going to be a long time before she saw such lush green again and breathed such pure air.

'I am going back myself tomorrow,' Nicholas said as he broke the not unfriendly silence. 'There is nothing more I can do here.'

'Where are you stationed?' she asked him.

'Biggin Hill.'

'Oh.' She knew it was one of the more important airfields around London.

'Are you going to be in London, Laura?'

She looked up at him, there had been a note in his voice which held an overtone of loneliness in it.

'Yes, for the time being. I shall be at the Woolwich barracks, but I expect to have another overseas posting soon.'

'If I've got leave and can't get to Hayle, do you mind if I look you up?'

Their eyes clashed. His dark look seemed to offer both apology and appeasement, and Laura felt a sudden irresistible urge to say yes; to see him again and to get to know him better.

'Why, yes, I should be pleased, Nicholas. I will give you the address of my flat in Bayswater. And, please, if you have any news of Christopher, will you let me know?'

He nodded. 'I expect you will hear before we do,' he said. 'I'm sorry he's not been in touch, Laura, it's very hard on you.'

'It's hard on your mother, too. I expect he will suddenly turn up out of the blue and she will be happy.'

'I'm going to try and get in touch with him through the War Office to let him know about Father, but of course, it could take months.' He put out a hand and took both of hers in his; the touch stirred her to look into his eyes and she found sympathy there. All previous animosity had vanished and Laura had the strange feeling that she had known him a long time.

'May I kiss you, Laura?'

She was startled into silence and before she had a chance to reply, he had leaned towards her and touched her lips with his in a kiss which was gentle and firm and meaningful all at the same time.

Then he was smiling at her. 'Thank you, Laura, that was very nice. I am glad you came, especially for Mother's sake, and I hope it won't be too long before you and I can meet again.'

Trying to forget the kiss, Laura knew that here was her chance to speak of his mother's worries, but she hardly knew if she dared; it would seem like interfering. But his mood was so different from what it had been that first day, she thought she would risk it for Jocelyn's sake.

'Your mother seems to be worried that she will have to leave Hayle House now that it is yours, Nicholas . . .'

She was allowed to go no further.

'Mother leave Hayle? Whatever is she thinking of? I haven't had a chance to talk to her, but will do so right away if she is worrying. It didn't occur to me, and I have been so busy trying to find someone to run the estate that I have hardly seen her. Poor dear; she can

128

continue just as she always has done if she wants to, for Marcia seems to like the flat and would never have the time to run the house as Mother does. If we have children, of course, we will have to think again, but for the time being there is no need for changes. I will talk to her as soon as you have gone.'

A wave of relief went through Laura; she was glad she had spoken and no more was said. Back in the house, Jocelyn had coffee ready for them and goodbyes were said and promises made. Laura left the big house more happily than she had entered it.

Back in London, she settled down to a routine of shifts at the hospital at the Woolwich barracks. She got used to the night duties and travelling home through a London still burning from a night of bombing, devastation everywhere, roads closed and the sickening shock of an unexpected gap where previously there had been a house.

When she was on days, she soon settled down in the evenings with the wireless or a book before the nightly ritual of the siren and the retreat to the cellar. On days off, she would sit in one of the parks or attend a midday concert at the National Gallery; she found it surprising that so many normal things could go on.

Her work at the hospital was routine and varied, her patients young, many of them raw recruits who had been injured during training.

All the young soldiers were impatient at the progress of the war, not knowing where trouble might flare up next.

September came and the evenings got darker and still Laura had no news from Christopher; one of her biggest consolations during that time was the regular weekly letters from Jocelyn. They were friendly letters and full of local news, and Laura was happy to reply.

At the end of one stint of night duty, she was given three days off and was glad to sleep most of the time. Now nearing the middle of September, the afternoons and evenings were getting chilly, but Laura still enjoyed her walks in the park amidst trees turning from green to gold and making their first scattering of leaves on the ground.

One evening, she was listening to a concert on the wireless when she thought she heard the sound of steps on the staircase up to the flat. Involuntarily she stiffened, as it was most unusual for her to have a visitor in the evening; her heart beat erratically and she felt an excited but nervous fluttering in her stomach as she wondered if it might be Christopher.

She went to open the door at the firm knocking and gave a gasp when she saw standing there not Christopher, but Nicholas Leybourne.

'Nicholas!' she cried out, and he laughed aloud at her astonishment and held out his arms to her. It seemed natural to run into them and she was gathered into a big hug and kissed softly on the lips.

'Am I allowed to kiss my sister-in-law?' he asked jokingly. 'I still remember the last kiss at Hayle.'

He stood looking down at her and she thought he was more handsome than she remembered; the lines of strain and worry had gone, and he looked young and dashing in his RAF uniform.

'I thought you would be Christopher,' she confessed.

'And are you disappointed?' His voice still held that note of laughter and pleasure.

'No, of course not, Nicholas, but what are you doing here?' She pulled up a chair for him, and when she sat down again she found her hands held closely in his; she did not pull away, she liked the contact and his nearness.

'I've got twenty-four hours,' he told her. 'It's not long enough to go home, so I thought I would look you up. You did give me permission, and I'm lucky to find you here. You've not been posted abroad again, then?'

She shook her head. 'No, worse luck, I've been wishing for some action. It's rather a strange war at the moment.' She looked at him; were his eyes tired? 'Are you still at Biggin Hill, Nicholas? Your war has never ceased, has it, in spite of the lull in the fighting?'

'No, as long as the Luftwaffe are sending bombers over, then we need our fighters.'

'Are you flying every night?'

'More or less, just the odd day off like today. But I've got a marvellous bunch of lads, so I can't grumble. However, I've not come to talk about the war, we've got to forget it for an hour or two: I want to take you out to dinner, Laura. Can you lend me a bed for tonight?'

She was all smiles; Nicholas seemed so different from the objectionable man who had greeted her in Yorkshire.

'Yes, of course you can stay, you can have Dorothy's bedroom. She's my sister who's down in Somerset with her school.' She looked at him. 'I'd like to change into something decent, Nicholas.'

'Yes, of course, and if you don't mind, I'll have a quick wash. Then we'll have to try and get a taxi, or are we near enough to the West End to walk in? It's still early evening so it will be safe; how about walking in and taxi back?'

'Lovely, I'll go and get changed.'

Laura felt as excited as a young girl getting ready for her first date. She put on a favourite dress of fine blue wool with pearls its only ornament, and flung a white jacket round her shoulders.

'You look lovely,' said Nicholas when she returned to the sitting-room. His hands touched her shoulders and he buried his face in her hair. 'Smell nice, too. I'm sure that

Christopher won't mind. Any word from him, by the way?'

'No, nothing, but your dear mother has written to me every week. Isn't it kind of her?'

'I think the kindness is the other way round, Laura; you write to her as well, and to her it's a link with Christopher, it means a lot to her.'

The walk into the West End took them half an hour, but it was a fine night and there was something exhilarating about walking in the dark with the searchlights sweeping the skies above. None of the menace of the later hours was there and to Laura, her hand loosely clasped by Nicholas, it seemed a happy breathing space between the rush of the day's work and the tensions that would come once the sirens had sounded.

Nicholas took her to a small restaurant not far from Baker Street, where he seemed to be well known. It was not crowded and the food was excellent; Nicholas ordered wine which seemed the greatest of luxuries to Laura.

He was surprising her with every word he spoke until she could hardly believe that this was the same Nicholas she had encountered at Hayle House. It was as though he had put off all cares just for that evening. Perhaps that is what we must do in times of war, she thought; if we didn't relax and put it behind us once in a while, the awfulness of it all would wear our spirits down.

In the taxi on the way home, he took her

hand and it was not the first time since she had known him that the touch had stirred her feelings.

'Thank you for coming out with me, Laura,' he said. 'I don't know when I've enjoyed an evening more; we need these times, you know, they are very important to us.'

He was echoing her own thoughts and it came to her how very much in tune with each other they were. During the evening they had found many common interests, especially a love of music; he admitted that Marcia only liked dance music and he had no liking for dancing. It was the only time that Nicholas mentioned Marcia and Laura again had that feeling of a distance which was almost an estrangement between the couple; it seemed that indeed all was not well with the marriage.

Now, in the darkness of the cab, she turned to him. 'I've enjoyed it, too, Nicholas, it's the first evening out I've had since . . .' She stumbled over her words.

'Since you married Christopher?'

'Yes, it does seem so long ago and sometimes I even wonder if I imagined it all; to be truthful, sometimes I even wonder if he is still alive.'

The grip on her hand tightened. 'We would have had official word if he had been killed, Laura; he will suddenly turn up as large as life, I know Christopher.'

The words dropped into a heavy silence and

134

Laura found she could only whisper. 'I don't, do I? Know him, I mean.'

'Don't worry about it, my dear girl; he will come back and you will be able to make a new start and all will be well. I wish I could say the same of *my* marriage.'

'Nicholas.' Laura was startled at the bitter tone in his voice.

'I'm sorry, I shouldn't have said that. Marcia and I haven't been getting on very well, but it's probably this bloody war. It's enough to wreck any marriage, never being at home and not knowing what's going on.'

It was getting late as they reached the flat and Laura was not surprised to hear the wail of the siren. She had told Nicholas of the arrangements in the cellar and they hastily put their coats on and went downstairs.

Laura made the introductions to the rest of the household and it seemed to cheer them all to have a visitor. She and Nicholas sat close together on a wooden bench, and when the bombs started to fall he put an arm round her shoulders and drew her closer to him. She found the contact both comforting and exciting; it seemed to be the most natural thing in the world to be sitting with him.

When the moment came that the cellar seemed to shake and they were deafened by an exploded bomb, Laura thought that they must have received a direct hit. She clung to Nicholas, daring to look up at him only when it became quiet.

It was only the slightest movement of her head, but he had bent towards her at the same time and their lips met. He had kissed her before, but this time it became a long moment of passion; Laura did not want that moment to end, but as thought took the place of sensation, she pulled her head away and murmured his name.

'Nicholas.'

'My dearest Laura.'

Then the enchantment seemed to end as the world righted itself and all of them in the cellar realized that they had not been hit and that they were still safe.

Upstairs again in the flat, Laura still felt shaky, and not only from their narrow escape, but also from that moment of heady contact when Nicholas had kissed her. She tried to sound practical and poured him a drink from Dorothy's precious bottle of brandy.

'It was a near one, Nicholas,' she said.

'Yes, we've been lucky . . .' He paused. 'I've had my eyes opened tonight, Laura.'

'Whatever do you mean?' she asked nervously, half sensing his meaning.

'It has been the whole evening, getting to know you and then . . . ?'

Remembering the kiss and the emotion she had felt, Laura thought she must interrupt quickly before they became too involved with their feelings.

'I will show you Dorothy's bedroom,' she said hastily, and walked to the door.

'I don't think I want to see Dorothy's bedroom tonight.'

Laura turned in astonishment and sought his eyes to question his words.

She found his gaze upon her, and the intensity of his expression caused her to give a shiver which was part apprehension and part excitement as she wondered at his meaning.

'What are you saying, Nicholas?' she managed to say.

His next words came with a clarity both intentional and purposeful; he knew exactly what he was saying and what he was meaning to say.

'I want to sleep in your bed, Laura, with you.'

CHAPTER SIX

Laura stood immobile by the door, not knowing which emotion had struck her most forcefully, shock or disbelief, or confusion and then an unbelievable sense of excitement.

As her mind cleared, she pushed the conflicting feelings to one side and thought only of realities.

They faced one another as Nicholas came near, Laura longing for that nearness while at the same time rejecting it with the logic of her thoughts.

'I am going to ignore that last statement, Nicholas, as you cannot be serious. I am married to Christopher and you have Marcia.'

The words sounded feeble against the intention in his dark eyes, the domination of his tall figure.

'Be damned to convention.' The words exploded from him. 'Your marriage to Christopher is a myth and you know it, and mine to Marcia foundered a long time ago when I went into the RAF. Come here.'

She was mesmerized and took a step towards him. He did not touch her and spoke slowly and softly.

'You are very beautiful, Laura; this evening has been an enchantment and I want it to end in love.'

'But you do not love me, Nicholas.'

'No, I cannot say that I do, it would not be honest, but I am very near to loving you. I have yet to know you, and I have no wish to spoil things between you and Christopher. But in the same way as this evening I have got to know some of your thoughts, now tonight I long to know your body.'

'Nicholas, stop it, stop it. What are you saying?' Laura was startled by his frank words, but did not seem to have the power to turn away.

He put out a hand and took hers and led

her to the settee where, without thought, she sat at his side.

His fingers were under her chin, tilting her head up to his, and she waited for his kiss without protest. It was long, it was exploring, it was sensuous; when his fingers moved to the buttons of her dress, she did not want to stop him. His hand slid under the soft wool and when she felt the gentle caressing of her breasts, a throbbing sensation pulsed through her whole body. At that moment, she wanted nothing more in the world than to be one with him.

He was saying things she could not hear or understand; he was leading her into the bedroom and she was hardly aware that she had moved; gently, he undressed her, touching her everywhere with soft lips and fingers until she buried her head in the pillow with a wild longing in her body.

She was prepared for roughness from him, recognizing his urgent need. But this big man did not hurry her; slow movements as smooth as silk brought her to a peak of sensation and she cried out for the final satisfaction. He came to her deeply then and Laura knew that she was experiencing the ultimate in the act of love for the first time.

He kissed her tears, repeating her name and calling her his love. They lay together quietly until both drifted into a sleep from which Laura was roused to find that it was first light and that she was alone. But only for seconds; suddenly Nicholas was at her side, dressed in his air force blue and smelling freshly of shaving soap. He covered her naked body with the sheets and dropped a kiss on her forehead.

'Laura, my dearest girl,' he whispered. 'I hardly know what to say, except to thank you for the magic we somehow made together. I hope it was magic for you, too. We have to go our separate ways now, and next time we meet, no doubt it will be as brother and sister-in-law; but nothing can take last night away from us. It was a glorious oasis in this infernal war and all I can say is thank you, Laura. Now I must go, for I am required to report for duty at nine o'clock.'

Laura lay there smiling, she did not attempt to move. She had listened to his words with a great feeling of pleasure and felt no disappointment; she understood all he was trying to say.

'I will never forget, Nicholas, and I promise not to feel guilty. I know I have been unfaithful to Christopher, but my feelings last night gave me no choice; it all seemed so right and perfect and I will never forget.'

'Bless you and God protect you.'

'You, too, Nicholas. Goodbye.'

'Goodbye, Laura.'

And he was gone.

Laura dreamed her way through the next two hours while she bathed and dressed and had breakfast. She must try and forget Nicholas even though for ever he would be part of her immediate family, but just for a few moments, she would allow herself to dwell upon the magic he had spoken of. She would think of the night that was past and not of the day to come.

For that day would soon be here and once she was at the hospital, back on the wards, reality and common sense would return to her; life would be back to normal and, once again, she would be writing to her mother-in-law and waiting in vain for news of Christopher.

Life did return to normal, if normal can describe the nightly sojourn in the cellar, the constant effort to make meals from meagre rations and the continual turnover of young soldiers on the wards. She found that their cheerfulness of spirit was an example to all and an encouragement to the nurses who cared for them.

A month later and within the space of three days, Laura's world was suddenly to turn upside-down. She did not see any more of Nicholas, but received a letter from him which she treasured; he seemed to want to make up for the lack of news from Christopher and told her that he wanted to write to her to prove that not all the Leybourne men were bad correspondents. He was desperately tired after ten nights in the air without a break, but he was determined she should know that her beauty and her generosity had transformed his life; in any other circumstances, he told her, he was sure that he would have come to love her very much. As it was, he was pleased to think that she was going to be his sister-in-law and that he would for ever be able to be close to her.

It was on the same day that this letter arrived that Laura heard from QA headquarters that she was to join the SS *Crediton* at Tilbury on 20 October, destination unknown.

She was given three days' leave by the hospital and knew that she just had time to go and see her parents before she sailed. She was, in fact, packing her case when she received the unexpected phone call.

She answered the phone, as always wondering if it would be Christopher; but it wasn't, it was his mother.

'Laura, this is Jocelyn.' Her mother-in-law sounded excited. 'Laura, my dear, such exciting news. Christopher has asked me to ring you; he's here, he arrived late last night, tired out. He is still asleep, so I promised I would ring you first thing. Can you come, dear?'

'Oh, Jocelyn, I don't believe it. I've got a posting; I'm sailing on the twentieth, I was just going up to Cumberland for a few days.' Laura was agitated, she could scarcely believe that Christopher was home at last; she found herself trembling.

'Will your parents mind if you come here instead? Give them a ring and come up on the first train. Christopher will be up by then.'

They both laughed as Laura promised to travel up as soon as she could get a train. She phoned her parents, who were very understanding and almost as excited as Jocelyn; she took a taxi to the station and found herself lucky with the trains; there was an express to Edinburgh which stopped at York and she could change for Richmond there.

The faithful Joe Sleightholme was available and took her straight out to Hayle; it was two o'clock in the afternoon.

All the way in the train with its usual jostling crowd of troops, Laura had been lost in an anxious dream. She asked herself the same questions over and over again, though she knew she could not supply the answers until she arrived at Hayle. First of all, she even wondered if she would recognize Christopher, her memory of him was fleeting and dim; she remembered best his fair hair so much in contrast to Nicholas's dark brown.

And would he have changed, she asked herself? Where had he been? Would he have regretted his hasty marriage? As she saw the flat green fields of the Midlands speeding past and delighted in the changing colours of autumn, she tried to test her own feelings and knew only anxiety as she sped to the meeting with her husband of only two days.

As the car drove slowly up the drive to Hayle House, Laura felt a fluttering and a sickness in her stomach; her mouth was dry, but her hands were damp.

She paid Joe and he grinned, speaking his first and only words. 'Mr Christopher 'ome then, is 'e, miss?'

She climbed the steps of the porch and before she had time to knock, the door was opened by a smiling Mrs Maw.

'Here you are, Miss Laura, Mr Christopher will be pleased to see you.'

She was in the hall, there were footsteps running down the stairs and her name was called out loud.

'Laura, my darling Laura.'

She saw the flash of fair hair before she was caught in an embrace which she thought was going to crush her. Then she pulled away and looked at him shyly. The blue eyes were dancing, he looked tired, he also looked very young. He was the Christopher she remembered.

'Christopher.' There seemed no more to say.

'Laura, are you really my wife? Sometimes I thought I imagined it all. Oh, Laura.'

He kissed her then and Laura felt warmth and affection return as he held her close; the feeling was not earth-shattering, but she felt at home and experienced a sense of gladness.

He guided her into the drawing-room and they sat close together on the settee. 'Mother is getting some tea, but I am sure she will leave us on our own; we have so much to talk about.' His smile dropped from his face for a moment. 'I didn't know about Father, it was a terrible shock. I still can't quite believe it. Mother's wonderful, isn't she? You have been very kind to her, Laura, she has told me about it. I'm glad you came to Hayle.'

She smiled rather ruefully. 'I'm afraid I didn't arrive at a very good time, and you had told me nothing. Oh, Christopher, why didn't you tell me about Hayle, about your family?'

He was not to reply, for at that moment the door was opened and Jocelyn came in, carrying a tray of tea; there were only two cups and saucers.

Laura got up to kiss her mother-in-law and was given a warm greeting. 'Laura, my dear,' Jocelyn said, 'he is here at last and looking well in spite of his tiredness. I'm not going to intrude, for I know that the two of you will have a lot of talking to do. Christopher brought me up to date with his news last night.'

There was a silence when she left the room. Laura sipped her tea and felt awkward; this was her husband, but she didn't know what to say to him, but she need not have worried, for Christopher was more than eager to get

145

reacquainted with his wife.

'Laura, are you stationed in this country now? Mother says that you've been in London.' He paused. 'What is it, Laura?' He saw her frown and sensed that she had something urgent to tell him.

'Didn't your mother tell you? I've got a posting, Christopher, I've only got two days before I sail.'

His arm came round her and he kissed the top of her head. 'We are destined to meet just for a few hours before you sail off into the blue! We'll make the most of these two days, Laura; it will be our honeymoon. Where did you end up last time? Did you go to North Africa?'

'Yes,' she told him. 'Greece first and then a desert hospital until I got a fever and was sent home. I don't know where it's going to be this time. But you, Christopher, where did you go? And, Christopher . . .'—there was a hesitation in her voice—'why didn't you write? I didn't have a single letter and neither did your mother. What happened?'

He got up then and walked across the room to the French windows; Laura sensed that although he was looking at the flowers and staring beyond to the trees of the wood where she had sat with Nicholas, Christopher was seeing distant sights and views and was being transported back to places probably half-way across the world.

Then his voice came to her, but he did not turn his head. 'I'm sorry, Laura, I know I was in the wrong, but it was very difficult. In the first place, I knew you wouldn't be at the flat so how would any letters find you? But it wasn't only that . . .'

He did turn then and came and sat by her, taking her hands in his and holding them tight. 'I will tell you what happened after I'd said goodbye to you; can you bear to listen?'

'Please, Christopher, I want to know all about it.'

'My foot soon healed and I got my posting. It was to India. Not the lovely India of the tea-planters; we were stationed just outside Bombay and it was foul. The heat didn't suit me, conditions weren't very hygienic and my foot got infected. It took months to get it right again and I was feeling beastly low; we all were. In fact, it didn't seem to have anything to do with the war, being stuck in that rotten country; it was all so futile. How could I write and tell you all that? How could I write to Mother? I've tried to explain to her, and I think she understands, she is very forgiving. Will you be forgiving, too, Laura?'

He had framed her face in his two hands and she found herself looking into worried blue eyes.

She had to smile at him. 'Of course I understand; now that you are safely here it is all forgotten. I think the worst part was not knowing if you were all right or not.' She felt his lips touch hers, lightly and briefly, almost with a feeling of uncertainty.

He got up, suddenly restless, still partly in the past. 'Come on, let's go for a walk before it gets dark. I want to put it all behind me, I want to realize that I am back at Hayle, I want to be really sure that I've got you by my side.'

They put on coats and Laura retraced her steps down to the wood, this time her hand firmly clasped by Christopher, neither of them saying anything as though perhaps just the physical contact would bring them back together again.

They sat on the seat and Laura found that the view across the dale had changed with the season; the greens replaced by gold, and a cool wind stirring the branches and bringing the leaves down.

Christopher turned to smile at her. 'Have you been here before, Laura? It is always a favourite place of ours.'

Laura tried desperately not to register on her face the surge of feeling which went through her at the question, for it was not the last time she had come here that she was remembering, but the last time she had been with Nicholas. She felt herself go hot and was sure that her face was red, but she tried to speak calmly.

'Yes, Nicholas brought me here. I'm afraid he wasn't very pleased to see me when I suddenly turned up; he wouldn't even believe that I was your wife. But, of course, afterwards I discovered how upset he was at your father's death.'

'Always did take things seriously, did Nicholas; we aren't a bit alike, you know. I suppose I take after Mother and Nick is more like Father.'

'You don't even look alike; no one would take you for brothers.' Laura could feel the tenseness of the moment slipping away and was relieved that they were getting on to more comfortable ground. But then she remembered Meg.

'Oh, Christopher, I met Meg, too.'

His horrified reaction was genuine. 'Christ, I'd forgotten about Meg. I think I got engaged to her or something, though it was a silly thing to do, I realize that now. She was more like a sister to me. Was she very upset?'

Laura shook her head. 'The family were more upset than Meg until they found out the truth. Everything is fine; Meg has met someone else, too, so I think it was a relief to her to find out that you had got married. We got on very well, I liked her.'

He turned and took her in his arms, looking down into her eyes. 'And are we going to get on very well, Laura?' he said softly.

'Oh, Christopher, I do hope so.'

His kiss wasn't brief this time, neither was it gentle and Laura gave herself up to the months of longing and waiting and loneliness that he had gone through.

As the embrace ended and Christopher whispered words of love, Laura was dismayed to find herself near to tears with a fluttering of weakness in her stomach. But then she saw the sure signs of happiness in Christopher's face and tried to convince herself that if she could make him happy, then there was a chance that their marriage could be successful.

They stayed there for a long time, renewing their friendship and talking over their experiences. While Laura felt encouraged by their light-hearted exchange, she also felt a haunting nostalgia for the last conversation she had had with Nicholas and guiltily she weighed up the differences between the two brothers.

At dinner that night, there were just the three of them, Laura, Christopher and his mother; Marcia was missing and Jocelyn said that she quite often stayed at the farm for her evening meal, a habit she had got into during the summer months when haymaking and harvesting could be carried on until very late in the evening.

The two days passed in a flash and Laura felt herself to be in a strange mood; she was enjoying Christopher's company and, during the day, all was well between them. Come the night, in the large guest-room which Jocelyn had given them, Laura found herself unmoved by Christopher's quick impulsive acts of love and, once again, memories would not leave her. As she lay awake unfulfilled after Christopher had fallen into an immediate sleep, it was of Nicholas she thought. She knew it was wrong and she hoped the memory would fade, but at that moment Nicholas's powerful and sensual persuasions filled her mind and her senses.

Another strange anxiety filled those brief two days, though for most of the time she managed to put it out of her mind: her period was overdue and she was often conscious of a faint queasiness as though she were sickening for something, but she realized that her system had undergone a shock with Christopher's sudden return, and she put her sick feelings down to the fact that she still felt a slight nervousness in her relationship with her husband.

But on that first morning, she was glad of the autumn sunshine and glad of the chance of being out of doors in beautiful surroundings for a little while.

At breakfast, Christopher asked what she would like to do; he could not take her far because of the shortage of petrol.

Laura had little hesitation. 'Do you think we could walk round the Hayle estate?'

He looked at her in astonishment. 'Is that really what you would like to do?'

'Yes, I would,' she replied. 'I would like to

visit the farms and walk as far round as we can manage so that I can go away and be able to imagine it all.'

Jocelyn was smiling in agreement. 'I think it is a lovely idea of Laura's, and Mrs Peacock and Mrs Hird would love to meet her; they are the wives at the two farms, Laura.'

It was a very successful venture. Laura was taken through fields, into woods, and they climbed to the highest point of the estate which looked over the River Swale, a silvery glint way below them. They found Mr Peacock of Holme Farm ploughing and he sent them to the farmhouse so that Mrs Peacock could give them coffee. Both Mr and Mrs Hird were home at Hayle Farm and more than pleased to see Christopher again and to meet his new wife.

They left the farm and, as Hayle House came into view, Christopher put an arm around her shoulders.

'Well, now you have seen Hayle. Will you like living here, Laura?'

She looked at him quickly. 'It's all quite beautiful, but you don't mean that we'll live in the house, do you? I don't think Marcia would like that; in fact, she told me that she wouldn't.'

'She did, did she? That sounds like Marcia.' But he said no more on the subject. 'It's no good looking into the future; you are off abroad again and God knows where my next posting will be. Anything can happen. But it's enough for me to know that you'll be happy up here in the wild north and won't pine for the lights of London.'

Laura smiled. 'Not me, I think I'm a country girl at heart. You will be going back into the firm, Christopher? After the war, I mean?'

'Yes, I shall have to. Nicholas will have his hands full with the farms and the estate, but I think he will like that. I hope that nothing happens to either of us for Mother's sake; she has suffered enough losing Father so suddenly.' His arm tightened on her shoulders. 'We were right to get married, weren't we, Laura? It wasn't a mistake, you are happy, aren't you? I love you very much.'

Laura was glad she didn't have to meet his eyes. 'I'm sure that we did right, Christopher, I love you, too.'

And Laura knew that she was lying.

But she was never to regret her words and as they reached the drive, she laughed with him when he insisted on running the rest of the way up to the house. They arrived breathless to find an amused Jocelyn waiting for them and lunch on the table.

Laura was glad to see Jocelyn so happy and cheerful that lunchtime, even though she could sense the underlying sadness that Robert was not there to see his son safely home. Talk was all of the past and it was pleasant to hear of times before the war and interesting for Laura to learn about the family she had married into.

Christopher disappeared as they rose from the table, and Laura helped Mrs Maw with the washing-up and then carried coffee through to Jocelyn who was sitting in the drawing-room. Laura found her putting a match to the log fire; the days were getting colder and she had already noticed a sense of chill about the big house.

Jocelyn smiled as Laura went into the room. 'At least we don't have to worry about coal rationing at Hayle. I think there's enough dead wood about to keep us going for a hundred years.' And she pointed to the gleaming brass cauldron full of dried-out logs. 'What are you and Christopher going to do with yourselves this afternoon?'

Laura shook her head. 'I don't know, he mentioned something about seeing the dale and now he's gone off somewhere.'

'Probably gone to look at his beloved car, though it's no use to him without petrol!'

But within five minutes, Jocelyn was proved wrong as Christopher appeared, breathless and excited as a small boy. 'Laura, come on. I've got the car going, dear old thing'

'But what about petrol, Christopher?'

'I ran back to the farm and Peacock let me have a can. Would you like to see something of the dale, Laura? I can't take you far, but we must try and show you some of the local beauty spots.'

'It would be lovely, but what about your mother?' she replied, looking at Jocelyn.

But Jocelyn was shaking her head. 'It is kind of you to think of me, Laura, but I want you two to have some fun on your own.'

When they got to the front steps, Laura found the smallest two-seater she had ever seen, gleaming black and without a hood.

Christopher grinned. 'Bates has kept her polished, isn't he a marvel? Have you met him?'

Laura nodded. 'Your mother said he was gardener, stableboy, chauffeur and odd-job man all rolled into one; she said that if he were a woman, he would be described as a "treasure"!'

'She is quite right. Now you go and get a coat, and you'll need something on your head, Laura, it will be a bit breezy.'

Laura ran back to get her coat and a headscarf and squeezed into the seat beside Christopher. With a wave to Jocelyn, who was all smiles, they roared down the drive.

'We'll go down to Marske first and I'll show you where Meg lives. I think I'd better go and see them tonight; will you mind, Laura? You can come, too.'

'Yes, I'd like to see Meg again before I go,' she replied, then concentrated on seeing as much of the countryside about her as the speed of the little car would permit.

They drove past Clapgate Lodge, then

155

Christopher sped down a very narrow lane into the small town of Reeth, the gateway to Swaledale. They had a walk round and Laura liked its sloping wide green and its cluster of cottages, shops and small country inns.

Christopher had his arm around her shoulders as they walked back to the car. 'Just enough petrol left to take you up the hill and show you the view up the dale.'

Above Grinton, he made her get out again and they walked to the moor where the wind was blowing hard and Laura was glad of her scarf.

As she looked, she felt tears come to her eyes for before her, the whole of Swaledale opened out; she could see the steep slopes of the hills and, lower down, the patchwork of fields and grey stone walls; each field had its stone barn, and here and there were groups of buildings which made up the farms and villages which stretched up the dale from Reeth.

Christopher was pointing out the landmarks. 'Beautiful, isn't it, Laura, our little part of the world?'

Still feeling emotional and tearful, Laura felt that wherever she was sent, this was how she would remember England. 'Yes, it is beautiful, Christopher, thank you for bringing me. I shall always remember that, wherever I am, I will have it to come back to.'

He turned her round in his arms and kissed

her. 'You are the beauty, Laura; I shall remember this moment, too; the land I have known all my life has now got you in it, and that makes it doubly precious.'

Laura looked at Christopher; she had never before heard him speak in such a way and she wondered if she had misjudged him. Their conversations had always been light-hearted nonsense with Christopher inclined to joke; she had not suspected a vein of serious thought in him. She reached up and kissed him and they made their way back down the hill, laughing as their feet slipped on the loose stones of the track.

The little car was soon speeding back along the lanes to Hayle House. As Laura let herself in the front door, she heard sounds of laughter in the hall and knew that it was Meg.

Inside, she found Marcia and Meg, still in their boots; they were talking to Jocelyn.

'Hello, Meg,' she said. 'Christopher is just putting the car away. He took me up the dale to see the views.'

Meg came up and kissed her. 'I am pleased you are here, Laura; I've come to give something back to Christopher.' She held out her hand and in it glistened the blue stones of a sapphire ring. 'It's my engagement ring. I knew it was a family ring so I want him to have it back. Jocelyn says it belonged to Christopher's grandmother.'

'He'll be pleased to see you, Meg; we were

going to walk over tonight.'

At that moment, Christopher arrived on the scene and his lively eyes took in the group of people standing there.

'Meg.' His voice was full of gladness.

The short girl turned round and shrieked his name, then flew into his arms. Laura smiled at the sisterly hug, glad that there was no ill-feeling between them.

'Meg, you've forgiven me then?' Christopher asked before he turned and took Laura's hand.

'Oh, Chris, I'm very pleased. Did Laura tell you about Rob? We are going to be married on his next leave.'

He laughed out loud. 'We've both been unfaithful, haven't we? But I'm very pleased it's turned out well and I hope you will be very happy.'

'I've got your ring, Chris, I thought you would like it back . . .' She hesitated for a moment and then held it out to him.

'Thank you, my dear, it was Grandma Leybourne's.' He turned to Laura. 'This seems awful, Laura, but would you like to have it until I can buy you a proper engagement ring?'

Laura let him put it on her finger. 'I'd be thrilled, and you don't have to buy me a new one. I like old jewellery which has been in the family.'

They all went into the kitchen for some tea and even Marcia was amiable; Laura thought that she behaved with more friendliness to Christopher than she did to her own husband.

Laura felt tired and happy after Meg had gone, and she was helping Jocelyn to wash the cups in the kitchen; it had been a nice day and her tiredness surprised her a little; she was usually a person of boundless energy, used to hard work with very little sleep.

Suddenly she noticed that Jocelyn was looking at her keenly. 'Are you all right, Laura? You are looking pale.'

Laura laughed. 'I do feel a bit tired,' she confessed. 'And don't tell Christopher, but I don't think that his little gem of a car did much for my stomach. I felt a bit sickly coming home down the lanes, but it's nothing and we can have a quiet evening now that we have seen Meg.'

Her mother-in-law turned back to the washing-up and didn't make any comment.

'I'm very pleased with my ring, Jocelyn, it's lovely, isn't it?' Laura continued. 'I like the old Victorian setting, it's got a lot of character. I hope Christopher doesn't buy me another one. You must tell him not to, Jocelyn.'

'I will, Laura. You are a dear girl and I bless the day that Christopher met you.'

That night, after a leisurely dinner and a stroll to the wood, Laura stood with Christopher in a darkened bedroom looking out on to a garden which was softly bright with moonlight. She was in her nightdress and he stood behind her with his arms around her; Laura felt a strange thankfulness that she was not aroused. Sometimes, she thought, I can hardly understand my own feelings.

But Christopher was speaking and she was glad of the friendly ease between them. 'I am sorry you to have to go, Laura, I feel that I've only just found you again. I must hope that it won't be such a long time before we see each other again. Neither of us knows where we'll end up but; God willing, we'll soon be safely back here at Hayle. The war can't last forever.'

'Do you think we'll be invaded?'

'Not as long as Hitler is fighting the Russians,' he replied. We ought to be landing troops in France, but we haven't got the strength. It's hard to see any outcome at the moment, and all the time there are innocent people being killed in air-raids and men like Nick risking their lives every night.'

Laura couldn't help herself, she felt a tremor go through her as Christopher mentioned Nicholas's name.

'You're cold, Laura, I'm a brute,' he said, his cheek on her hair. 'Into bed and I'll soon make you warm.'

He reached out to draw the curtains, and in total darkness Laura got into the big bed; she could sense his need for her and hoped with all her heart that she would be able to respond to his quick and eager caresses.

Afterwards, he slept contentedly and she

thought over the pleasant companionship of the day; she knew that she could do a lot worse than to be married to someone as kind as Christopher.

CHAPTER SEVEN

Two days later found Laura on the quayside at Tilbury looking in vain for other QA nurses. Then, when she found the *Crediton*, she discovered that it was quite a small liner and not the troop ship she had been expecting. She was about to board when she felt a hand on her arm and turned to find herself looking at a very tall and powerfully built man in the uniform of the RAMC.

His smile was friendly. 'I am on the lookout for QAs and you seem to be one of them,' he said. 'Have you seen any of the other sisters?'

'No, I've looked everywhere, I thought there would be quite a lot of us.'

'I am Dr Steven Franks. I think we will be travelling out together.'

Laura introduced herself. 'Do you know where we are going?' she asked him.

He nodded. 'Yes, I've got the orders. I'll tell you when we've found the others. Perhaps they are already on board; we'd better go and see.'

He helped her with her case and she followed him on to the liner. There were very few people about and it seemed strange. Dr Franks made enquiries and was directed to the sick-bay; again Laura followed and they soon found themselves opening swing doors into a large and airy medical room. Inside, three nursing sisters, in their scarlet and grey, were standing as though wondering what to do next. They turned at the sound of the door opening and their faces lit up with smiles when they saw the tall doctor.

He looked from one to another and smiled back, then he opened a case and took out a file of papers.

'I am Dr Franks,' he said, 'and I am going to be your MO for the trip. I will give you the details in a moment, but first of all we must make sure that you are all here and then you can introduce yourselves to one another if you haven't already done so.' He started reading from the piece of paper in his hand.

'Sister Anna Philips.'

A tall thin girl with a serious face put up her hand.

'Sister Gillian Knowles.'

An older person standing next to Laura indicated that she was Sister Knowles and Laura liked the look of cheerful common sense in a rather plain face under already greying hair.

'Sister Laura Leybourne, we've met already; and Sister Pamela Tulkinghorne.'

The last named was a short girl with fair

162

hair who reminded Laura of Jenny.

Dr Franks had shaken hands with each of them and they found enough chairs to be seated while they listened to what he had to say.

'My orders are that we are going to join the hospital that has been set up in Freetown, Sierra Leone. It is a British colony and a very important port and rail link; we have a brigade there and it is also an important port of call for the Atlantic run. I tell you all this so that you will recognize the strategic importance of Freetown in West Africa and of the value of the work that you will be doing there.' He looked around him and saw four serious faces.

'If you think it is a safe haven, I can soon disillusion you, for the enemy at Freetown is the climate. It is not for nothing that it became known as the "White Man's Grave" before the malarial swampland was filled up. Fortunately the hospital is built high up on Hill Station, which is the British part of the town. I've not been there myself, but I understand it is a healthy district with splendid views over the town. Now, I have said enough; are there any questions?'

Gillian spoke first. 'This liner, the *Crediton*, Dr Franks, we seem to be the only ones on it at the moment. Is it going to be a troop ship?'

'No, it will carry some army personnel who have been on leave and others who have business in Freetown and other places in West

163

Africa.'

'Will we have any duties during the voyage?' asked Laura.

'Yes, you will run this unit and cope with any illness or accidents which might occur, under my direction. Through those doors,' he said, pointing to another pair of swing doors at the opposite end of the room, 'there should be a small ward of four beds. I don't imagine we will need more, I certainly hope not. I'd better warn you that we are not sailing in convoy and will be open to attack from the air while we go through the Channel and from enemy submarines when we are in the Atlantic. Anything else?'

'Should we have had vaccinations?'

'That is all arranged and I will give them during the next few days. All the other passengers should already have had their vaccinations, but we'll have to do a check.' He looked at them again. 'Our cabins are supposed to be near, so shall we go and have a look?'

Laura somehow found herself walking with Gillian Knowles and it seemed only natural that they should go together into the first cabin which was indicated. The cabins were to be shared.

It was Gillian who spoke first. 'You're Laura, aren't you? Would you mind sharing with me, or would you rather be with one of the younger ones?' she asked.

Laura laughed. 'No, I'd love to be with you; it's not a bad cabin, is it?'

They looked around them and saw that it was small but comfortable with plenty of room to put their clothes and store their cases and bags.

'How do you feel about going to Freetown?' Gillian asked. West Africa is the last place I thought we'd be sent to.'

Laura was thoughtful. 'I'm not too happy about the climate. I had to be sent home from North Africa because of a fever, but perhaps if we're high up in the town we'll be OK. It's not like being in the desert.'

Gillian nodded sympathetically and they turned to their cases. 'I suppose we'd better get unpacked and then we'll go in search of the dining-room. It seems strange being on an empty ship.'

The ship did not stay empty for long, but it was a week before they sailed, and during that time they all got to know each other and to establish a routine. Two of them were always on duty at night and two during the day; Laura and Gillian stuck together and shared the shifts. They soon got to know and like each other.

It was well into that first week at sea that Laura found she had time to think; and she not only started to think, but also to worry, for it was during that time that she missed her second period. She had got used to her queasy feelings and associated them with the general upset in her life over the last few weeks. She expected to feel better now that they were settled on the *Crediton* and she was more certain of what the immediate future held.

But a few days out, and in the Channel with a blustery wind, Laura woke up, made a rush for the washbasin and was sick.

Gillian was beside her in a moment and led her back to her berth. 'Seasick, Laura? Are you a sufferer?'

Laura, feeling awful and wondering if she was going to have to make another dash, put a hand to her stomach. 'I've never been seasick in my life,' she told Gillian.

'Never mind,' said her friend. 'I'll mix something for you and bring you a plain biscuit. You'll be OK by breakfast-time.'

Laura couldn't eat breakfast, but the rest of that day she felt quite fit. The next three mornings were a repeat of the first, and Laura knew she had to come to terms with what was happening to her; she was also suffering from heartburn, and her breasts were heavy and tender. She knew she was pregnant, but was afraid to sit down with her diary and work out dates. It was Gillian who forced her to face up to the truth.

The bout of morning sickness over, Laura sat drinking the cup of tea which Gillian had brought her.

As the older woman handed over the cup

and saucer, she looked at Laura keenly. 'It's not seasickness, is it, Laura?' she said bluntly. 'You must be pregnant, but I don't quite understand. You told me that you had met up with Christopher immediately before you joined the ship. That's not that long ago; you can't possibly be this far advanced.'

There was a silence in the cabin and Gillian watched Laura struggling with her feelings, tears not far from the surface.

'I'm sorry, my dear, I've put my big foot in it, haven't I? I'll go and have my breakfast, and bring you another cup of tea and some toast. You need to be on your own, don't you? We don't get much privacy.'

Laura watched Gillian disappear from the cabin, and was thankful for her tact and kindness. For Gillian had spoken the truth and Laura knew it. She remembered vividly her first feelings of sickness and how she had put it down to the excitement of Christopher's return, and then how she had blamed his little car. She took her diary from her handbag and looked at the dates; she worked out her periods and knew she was over a month pregnant. No, it could not possibly be anything to do with Christopher; she was bearing Nicholas's child.

Her first instinctive feeling was of supreme joy; that those moments of pleasure and love in Nicholas's arms had produced a child, *their* child. But the elation was shortlived; it lasted no more than seconds as the reality of her situation forced her into an awareness of what she had done and of what was happening to her.

I'm expecting Nicholas's child! She almost cried the words aloud. My own brother-in-law, he is married to Marcia and I am married to Christopher, but it is not his child I am going to have. What shall I do, whatever shall I do? She panicked then and could not think clearly. She did not break down into tears, though she felt like sobbing her heart out at her predicament. When Gillian came back into the cabin, it was to find her with her head buried in her hands.

'Laura, are you all right?'

Laura looked at her and met kindness in the homely face of the older woman. I could tell Gillian, she said to herself; I can't keep it to myself, I shall go mad.

'I'm in a mess, Gillian, an awful mess. I can't think properly; do you mind if I tell you?'

'No, of course not, drink this tea and try to eat something.'

Laura obeyed like a child, and as she sipped the tea and ate the toast, she told Gillian of the night of the air-raid in London when Nicholas had called to see her and had stayed the night.

'And it is Nicholas's child?'

'Yes.'

'Oh my goodness, my dear girl, whatever are

168

we going to do?'

They were both silent, busy with their own thoughts; then Gillian finally spoke, slowly and thoughtfully. 'You could divorce Christopher, and Nicholas could divorce his wife, and then you could marry each other. But that's not the answer, is it? You could get rid of the baby.' She looked at Laura as she spoke and was not surprised to see the girl's head jerk up in shock and indignation.

'Gillian, how could you suggest such a thing?'

'Sorry, dear, I'm not suggesting it, I'm just going through the possibilities. I don't agree with abortion either.'

'No, I've made up my mind.' Laura jumped up and took Gillian by the shoulder. 'No one knows except you, Gillian, and I am certain that you wouldn't let me down. I'm not going to break up any marriages. I shan't tell Nicholas; he and Marcia will have children of their own after the war. I shan't tell Christopher the truth, either. I shall let him and the family think that it is his child; the dates are so close, it would be easy to make a mistake.' She stopped speaking and glanced at Gillian, who was looking worried.

'It's a lie you will have to live with all your life, Laura. Are you sure you are doing the right thing?'

'Yes, I am. I couldn't tell Christopher the truth, which is that I was unfaithful to him with his own brother, and I would rather that Nicholas was ignorant of it.'

Gillian took the younger girl's hand in hers. 'I'm not sure that you are right, but at least you seem to be positive about it. That is important, and after all, you know the people involved; I don't. I'll just have to help you through this period of sickness and sooner or later you'll have to tell Dr Franks.'

'I'll work as long as I can, Gillian. I can stay in Freetown for a few months before I need to go home.' Laura got up, picked up her red cape and white cap, and put them on. 'And, Gillian, thank you for your help, I will never forget your kindness. Now, we've got a day's work to do, though I must say that at the moment we're not working very hard, are we?'

Gillian smiled. 'We'll take it easy while we can; we'll probably have to make up for it once we get to Freetown.'

They did have to work hard, for by the time they were crossing the Bay of Biscay in very stormy weather, they had several very sick passengers; this, combined with one or two mishaps while the more stalwart tried to walk the decks during the rough weather, filled their small ward.

Laura thought that by the time they had reached the roughest part of the voyage, her own sickness was wearing off. She and Gillian had changed to a spell of night duty and she thought that this, too, had helped, for she began to feel well again. She had convinced herself that deception was the best plan and even began to think of the baby as Christopher's; she would write and tell Jocelyn the news as soon as they reached Freetown, she told herself.

The small liner had been fortunate through the Channel and had not attracted much gunfire from the air; there were bigger and more important targets for the Luftwaffe in the form of convoys of cruisers and troop ships. But once out in the Atlantic, they felt vulnerable; they were in the main shipping lane and prey to the dangers of attacks from U-boats. Dr Franks had got them to make up emergency medical packs for the lifeboats and a lifeboat drill was carried out every day.

As the weather got warmer and the sea got calmer, Laura enjoyed sitting on the deck and relaxing when she and Gillian were not on duty. Dr Franks often sat with her on these occasions and she got to know him quite well; it rather amused her to think that these evenings were a pleasant repeat of the evening walks with Dr Neale in the desert, though she did not have to fear romance or another proposal of marriage, for Dr Franks loved to talk about his wife and family. Gillian, too, was glad of the friendship, as she was often tired in the evenings and content to sit quietly in their cabin.

Madeira and the Canary Islands were soon

left behind and as they got closer to Sierra Leone, they began to feel a sense of security. It turned out to be false. In fact, the *Crediton* was midway between Dakar and Freetown when she was struck by a torpedo. It was in the early hours of the morning. Laura and Gillian were on night duty, sitting quietly in the small medical unit, drinking tea and chatting.

The impact of the torpedo was a sickening and sudden loud explosion, and they knew that they had been struck somewhere in the stern of the ship, for they found themselves forced off their chairs and sprawling on the floor in a room tilting at almost forty-five degrees. The lights went out and, in the darkness, they groped for the medical kits and tried to make their way on to the deck.

'Hang on to me, Laura,' shouted Gillian. 'Don't let go. We've got to get to the lifeboats.'

Dr Franks was at the door when they managed to force it open and he took them both by the arm; by that time, they guessed that the engine-room had been hit, for the throb of the motors had ceased and there was a smell of burning oil.

The lifeboat drill had paid off for there was no panic on the deck. Passengers wearing coats over their nightwear and clutching bags crowded the rail as the boats were let down.

It was then that Laura lost Gillian; she was clutching Dr Franks's hand and somehow she was separated from her friend. It was to be many days before Laura found out that Gillian was safe.

There was another explosion behind them, and they could see flames rising from the ship; at the same time, the liner started to list.

Immediately, Laura began to panic, a huge welling of sickness and fear as she remembered Dunkirk; once again, she thought she was going to have to jump into the water. But then, as the smoke got dense about them, she saw that a ladder had been lowered, and there was a scramble to get into the boats.

Dr Franks didn't let go of her for a second and she had never been so glad of the firm grip of a strong hand. At each step down the ladder she was sure she would slip, but somehow, amidst the heat of the fire, the stench of the burning oil, the shouts and cries from passengers and orders from crew members, they reached one of the lifeboats and climbed into it.

The small boat was crowded, but it was stable. Two members of the liner's crew were rowing away strongly from the blazing, sinking liner. When she looked about her, she saw that they were in convoy with three other of the ship's lifeboats, but even in the heavy seas they managed to keep together.

There was a lot of shifting about, but enough room was made for everyone to sit down. The sun was rising in the east and they all felt very thirsty. Then she felt rather than heard her name whispered in her ear and realized that Dr Franks had been calling her name.

'Laura, are you all right now?'

'Yes, thank you; I'm beginning to realize that we're safe. There's no sign of Gillian, is there, or the other two?'

'No, but I'm sure they'll be on one of the other boats; as far I could see, everyone got off safely before the ship went down. But we've got one or two injuries and burns, do you feel up to giving me a hand? I've got the medical box here.'

'Yes, of course. I can tear my cap into bandages, as well, if we need it.'

Having something to do restored Laura to a sense of sanity and usefulness. The two of them worked as quickly as they could, putting on dressings where they were necessary and tending to burns; their medical box was small, but adequate. They used sea water for bathing the wounds and although the salt stung badly, it had good healing qualities.

They lost count of the days and tried to forget about hunger and thirst. There was fresh water on board, but the ration per day was very little; all the food they had was cans of bully beef and dry biscuits and these were divided out morning and evening. As long as they made progress, morale was good even in the heat. Laura found, as in the desert, that it got very cold at night and while it was a relief to escape from the sun, she was glad to share Dr Franks's greatcoat with him after dark; he had grabbed it at the last minute.

She soon discovered that you couldn't share a coat with someone and continue to call them 'Doctor'. Dr Franks was kindness itself and insisted that she called him Steven. During the day, they continued to dress the wounds which were healing nicely; when evening came and they had their meagre supper, they talked together until it was time to settle down and try to sleep.

It was on the fifth day that, for some reason, she felt morose and lacking in hope. No sign of any ship, no sign of land; nothing but sun and sea and the occasional shark to keep them company. The nights were beautiful, and as she sat with Steven under the thick coat, she looked at stars she did not know and could not stop herself from sighing.

'That was a deep sigh, Laura, are you all right?' Steven asked.

'I don't know what it is; it's such a beautiful night, but how can we appreciate beauty when everything seems so hopeless?'

'I can appreciate beauty as long as I am looking at you, Laura.'

Laura laughed then. 'Steven,' she said indignantly, 'how can you say such things when we are filthy dirty and probably smelling to high heaven?'

He laughed, too, and pulled her against

him. 'That's what I love about you, Laura; you've got guts and a sense of humour, and you *are* beautiful. If I wasn't happily married already and you were single, too, I'd be proposing to you here and now in this most unromantic situation.'

'You can't be serious, but I love you, too, for all you have done for me these last terrible days. But sometimes I wonder if this is the end; if you and I will die together and will not end our lives, you with your wife and me with Christopher. Do you feel like that, Steven?'

'No, I'm an optimist. I'm sure we will be rescued or that soon we shall see the coast of West Africa.' He held her to him and pulled the coat tightly around them until they were cocooned from the others and from the world.

The next day, two things happened and a certain lethargy began to creep through the spirits of all those in the small boat, though the men continued to row as heroically as ever.

The first thing touched them all because they realized that they would have to reduce the food supply and would only be able to deal out one ration a day; the rowers would get more.

Steven had been bathing the backs of the rowers with sea water, and when he came back to Laura he was alarmed to find her sitting in the blazing sun with the coat wrapped around her.

'Laura, whatever is it? You can't be feeling

cold.' His tone was anxious.

'I feel shivery,' she replied, and he knelt by her side, feeling for her pulse.

'You told me you had a fever in North Africa,' he started to say.

'Yes, I'm wondering if it's a return of that. I wish we could catch sight of land or spot another ship. There seems no hope.' To her shame and annoyance, she felt the tears come into her eyes and she thought she was going to cry; she guessed that her condition was making her weepy.

'There are some malaria tablets in the medical kit, I'll put you on those. Do you think you can swallow them without water?'

'I'll try,' she whispered, and shivered again.

After that, she lost count of the days and never knew if it was the next day or a week later when a cry went up that there was a ship on the horizon. She did remember the men standing up and waving their shirts as the ship drew nearer; she was aware of Steven's constant care, and finally the joy of seeing the ship come alongside and put down a ladder.

Somehow she climbed up, Steven helping her all the way, and once on board they discovered that it was a Royal Navy vessel. Room was found for all those rescued, and they had the bliss of a cup of tea and a wash in clean water; the best news of all was that they were only a day out of Freetown.

Laura felt as though her legs would not

support her and was aware that Steven had carried her to the sick-bay of the ship. All was hazy after that; someone washed her and put her in a sailor's clean pyjamas, she felt the prick of an injection, she heard voices. She lost count of time, shivering and raging with fever alternately and being grateful for long cool drinks of water; then she thought she remembered being lifted on to a stretcher and had a recollection of the rumbling, bumpy wheels of a vehicle. She thought she heard Steven talking to someone with a softer female voice.

One night, she felt she was sleeping peacefully; limp and without the will to wake up, she wondered if she was going to die. Then she thought it was Steven she heard; the clarity of his glad tones seemed to penetrate her subconscious.

'She has gone into a natural sleep, thank God; we will see a change in the morning.'

Laura opened her eyes to a very bright light and saw by some miracle that she was in a hospital, in a small ward; she was on her own except for a figure in the familiar grey and red, bent over a glass trolley near the door.

She tried to speak, but no sound came though her head had made a slight movement and the person across the room sensed it. In a flash, she was by the bed and Laura saw that it was Gillian.

'Laura, oh, Laura.'

'Gillian, where am I, what are you doing here?'

'Shhh, don't talk, you are in the hospital in Freetown, but I must go and tell Dr Franks that you are awake. He told me to tell him immediately; he is out on the big ward.'

Laura shut her eyes again; she was in Freetown, Steven was here and so was Gillian. Then she felt a hand on hers, looked up, and met Steven's smiling eyes.

She smiled, too. 'Steven,' she whispered. 'Have I been a worry to you?'

'You have, young lady, but I knew you were over the worst last night and the fever has gone at last. Do you think you could drink a cup of tea? We've got to start feeding you up now. Gillian is here, you know; she was on one of the other boats and she found us straight away . . .' He stopped, seeming hesitant. 'Or don't you remember? We were at sea in a lifeboat when you became so ill, then we were rescued and brought here. I don't know what I would have done without Gillian these last few days.'

'Yes, it is all coming back to me . . .' Her voice seemed to fade into a question.

He looked at the pale face of the girl in the bed and thought he saw the beginnings of a worried frown. 'What is it, Laura? Something is bothering you.'

'The baby, Steven, have I lost the baby?'

'No; by some miracle, the baby has survived.

179

But you didn't tell me that you were pregnant, Laura.'

She shook her head. 'No, it wasn't the time or place and I didn't know what was going to happen, but I'm very glad.'

Gillian appeared with some tea and Steven helped Laura to sit up; gratefully, she drank the tea and then lay back on the pillows and slept again.

She spent a week sleeping, then having a light meal and a few words of chat with Gillian or Steven, then sleeping again. At the end of that time, she began to feel stronger and they let her sit out each day. It was the beginning of the rainy season in Freetown, a bad time for cases of malaria, and Gillian was busy on the big ward. Laura felt guilty that she was not able to play her part and wondered how soon she would have her old energy back again.

When she asked Steven, Laura had her first and only quarrel with him. She was up and dressed in her grey dress and scarlet cape, looking out of the window of her small room at the view over Freetown. The hospital was situated high up on Hill Station, and from there Laura loved to see the lush green of the trees of the busy port. She was impatient, not only to get back to work, but also to be able to go out and explore.

It was Steven's habit to come and sit with her for an hour in the evening when he was off duty and had eaten his meal, but was still on call. Laura looked forward to these visits and was determined to ask him about when she could go back on duty.

'How's my favourite patient today?' He always greeted her in the same way, and she smiled up at him.

'Getting impatient, Steven. When can I go on the ward? I know how busy they are from what Gillian tells me, and I feel I'm not pulling my weight.'

He looked older that day; his hair had more grey in it and there were lines on his face. He also seemed uncomfortable about something, for he did not meet her eyes when she asked her question, but instead he walked to the window and looked out at the heavy beating rain.

'I've got to talk to you, Laura,' he said, still without looking at her, and she was suspicious, not only of his words, but also at the tone of his voice.

'What is it, Steven? I'm better now; there's nothing wrong, is there?'

He turned away from the window and came to sit by her side, taking both her hands in his.

'I'm not happy about this tropical fever you keep getting; that's twice it's happened and I'm convinced that the climate doesn't suit you.'

Laura thought she could see trouble coming. 'It doesn't suit any of us; West Africa is notorious, but I hope you're not going to say

181

that I can't work.'

He pressed her hands. 'That's exactly what I am going to say,' he said. 'I want you home in England before Christmas.'

She stood up and pulled her hands away from his grasp. 'That's ridiculous, I'm quite fit for work; I'll be able to do another three or four months before I need to think about going home. You can't send me back, I'm determined to stay here.'

Steven seemed to be making an effort to sound reasonable. 'I don't want to send you back, Laura, I don't want to lose you, but I think it is in your best interests and you have to think of the baby.'

'No, Steven, I won't go and you can't make me. My orders come from QA headquarters in London, not from you.'

'I have to disagree. When we left England, I was given sole responsibility for the four of you and it is up to me to make the decision.'

She had not heard him sounding stern and heavy-handed before and it was not like the Steven she had come to know.

'But I can do the work, I know I can; I've always been fit and healthy—'

He interrupted quickly. 'Until you came out to Africa; Laura, it doesn't suit you. Surely you can see that?'

'I don't see it and I don't see why I should do what you say; you can't make me go back.' Her voice was raised in anger and resentment and she did not see the sorrow and anxiety on his face; she left him where he was sitting and stormed out of the room into the kitchen where she hastily put the kettle on and made tea. She was blinded by the tears caused by the quarrel and the things Steven had said.

Half an hour later, she was still sitting there in gloomy silence when Gillian came seeking her out.

'Laura.' The older woman sounded concerned. 'Whatever has happened to you and Steven? I can't get a word out of him and he's as sunk in gloom as you seem to be. What's it all about?'

Laura was glad to see Gillian; perhaps she would be able to persuade Steven to change his mind.

'He wants to send me back to England,' she said flatly.

'Oh.'

'You might say "oh", Gillian, but I'm better now and I can't wait to get back on the ward, but Steven's being obstinate and we've quarrelled.'

Gillian was looking at her friend sympathetically, but she knew that she was not in a position to pour oil on to troubled waters.

'Perhaps it is you who are obstinate, Laura.'

'Gillian!' Laura was outraged; she had been certain that Gillian would take her side.

'Calm down, calm down, and listen to what I have to say, and don't interrupt.' Gillian was in a domineering mood. 'When I finally found you here, you were very ill and Steven was worried out of his wits. You would have thought you were his wife, the way he behaved. I told him you were pregnant and it only made him worse. For days, we didn't know if you would live, we didn't know if you would lose the baby. You should have seen Steven's face when you turned the corner. He is *very* fond of you, Laura, and if he says that this climate is not suitable for you, then he is only thinking of your own good. You must listen to him, my dear; he doesn't want to lose you any more than I do, but I happen to think that Steven is right, this time.'

Laura was silent for a long time, then she got up and put her hand on Gillian's arm. 'Thank you, Gillian, thank you. I think I needed that. I'll go and find Steven.' It was all she said and she went in search of the doctor.

She found him eventually in the office at the end of the big fever ward; he was standing at the filing cabinet and there was no one else near.

'Steven.'

He turned abruptly, took one look at her face and held out his arms. She ran to him and he held her close; his strong hold told her that he desperately wanted her to understand.

'I'm sorry,' she said, looking up at him. 'But you didn't tell me how ill I'd been. I should have trusted you to do what was right, I

184

shouldn't have argued with you.'

'It's all right, Laura,' he said softly. 'I can understand that it's very disappointing for you. You see, I kept thinking of all that time in the lifeboat with hardly any food and not enough water, then the weeks of illness. You need to catch up on that and you won't do it working out here. It's hard here, Laura, even I feel tired. I don't want you to go, but I'm going to insist, you know.'

She nodded. 'It's all right, I won't object. I've had a long talk with Gillian and she has made me see sense. It's always nice to be back in England and perhaps I can get a job in a hospital there.'

'Laura.'

She looked at him and laughed; she knew what he was going to say.

'You are to go home to England and rest; go up to that lovely home of yours in Yorkshire and eat all the good food the farm can provide; let your mother-in-law take care of you. She will enjoy that, from what you have told me about her.'

Laura felt herself relax as she resigned herself to the idea. 'You are right; you have to be for you are older and wiser than I am and I have to take your advice,' she said seriously.

'You have to take your orders from me, young lady.'

'Yes, sir.'

They both laughed.

Two days later, Steven and Gillian waved goodbye to Laura as she stood at the rail of the *Ramsgate*, a cruiser which was part of a convoy travelling back to England. The voyage was uneventful and gave Laura time for thought; she realized, rather ruefully, that it was the second time she had been invalided home, but she tried to think about the future and not of what she had left behind.

CHAPTER EIGHT

Laura was never to forget the first days on the *Ramsgate*, for, during that time, the Japanese bombed Pearl Harbor and America entered the war. News and rumour flew around the ship and everyone was glued to the wireless; every news bulletin was listened to and discussed with great avidity and attention.

On one hand, there seemed to be a sense of dismay that the war was now world-wide, but others were more optimistic of a quick and successful end to hostilities if America was now joined to the Allies. Churchill and Roosevelt had signed the Atlantic Charter earlier in the year and there was close co-operation between the two leaders.

The journey home seemed to go remarkably quickly; there were very few passengers on board the liner and Laura was the only woman. She was glad to be quiet and left alone with her own thoughts; she was ever conscious of her pregnant state, but felt well as they sailed into cooler waters.

By the time they landed at Southampton, she had put on weight and was feeling fit. She found a hotel in the centre of the city and from there she made a lot of phone calls. QA headquarters told her to rest at home until after the baby was born and to contact them afterwards if she wanted to. Her parents told her to get the first train to Cumberland, and Jocelyn was thrilled to hear from her and said she would be welcome at any time; Laura did not tell her about the baby and learned that there had been no news from Christopher. The next day, she travelled up to Cumberland.

Her parents lived in a small cottage not far from Penrith. There was a village store and post office and one bus a week into the town; it amused Laura that her mother and father had settled down so happily after so many years spent in the London suburbs.

But quiet and rest were what Laura needed, and her mother seemed to want to wait on her hand and foot. Up until Christmas, Laura gave in gracefully, but once the festival was over, she knew she would have to make her plans for the future. She was writing regularly to

Jocelyn again, having told her about the baby as soon as she was settled in Cumberland.

Jocelyn was delighted with the news, and said that it would make her more than happy to have Laura living at Hayle and also that Christopher's child should be born there.

Laura had not told her mother all this, as she had the feeling that she would be expected to stay at home; but over the weeks, she discovered that Mrs Terrington was worrying about the lack of space in the cottage for both Laura and a small child and when told of Jocelyn's offer, she was delighted.

A week later, Laura was making a long and difficult journey across the Pennines and, after a tiring day, she was glad to be in Joe Sleightholme's car in the last light of a January afternoon, making her way out to Hayle.

Joe carried her case up the steps for her and she knocked on the door expecting a warm welcome from Mrs Maw.

The door opened; a tall, smiling, dark-eyed man stood there. Laura shrieked.

And amidst exclamation and laughter, she was in his arms; she felt his magnetism, she felt his lips on hers, she felt happy and incredulous.

Then she remembered; she knew that her deceit and her life of lies were to begin at this very moment.

'Laura.'

'Nicholas! Are you home on leave?'

Their arms round one another, they turned into the hall to be greeted by a voice and comment which were full of sarcasm and rancour.

'That was more than a brotherly reception, wasn't it?'

Laura jerked round to see Marcia standing at the foot of the stairs; the tall woman was dressed in classic tweed skirt and jumper; her hair, which Laura had always seen knotted back, swung loosely about her shoulders.

'Hello, Marcia; it was such a surprise to see Nicholas, and it's lovely to be here again.'

'I understand we have to congratulate you, Laura; congratulate you and Christopher, that is. He will be delighted at the news of the baby.'

Laura looked up at Nicholas; it seemed to her a brave effort on her part to do so, but she encountered a look which shocked her. His eyes were bleak and hard, all the welcoming warmth had gone; it's as though he's jealous, she thought. Oh, God help me, it's going to be difficult.

But the awkward moment was broken by the arrival of Jocelyn; she, too, had a big hug for Laura.

'How lovely to see you again, Laura, and looking so well. Welcome to Hayle. I hope you will be content to make it your home until Christopher comes back.'

They were standing in a group in the hall

and Marcia's barbed tongue made it uncomfortable for all of them.

'I think it is *my* place to welcome Laura, Jocelyn; you seem to forget sometimes that I am mistress of Hayle now.'

Laura heard the words and watched Jocelyn's face with horror; her mother-in-law seemed close to tears and Laura felt that she could have hit Marcia for her lack of feeling. But Nicholas took things in hand and Laura felt some relief when he led Marcia through to the drawing-room, quietly remonstrating with her and shutting the door behind them.

Laura was left with Jocelyn, who had recovered her composure.

'Leave your case, my dear, and come into the kitchen; we'll have some tea together. Try not to take any notice of Marcia, she seems to feel it because I am still living here, but where could I go?'

They sat together near the kitchen range and Mrs Maw, who was delighted to see Laura, made them tea.

'It's nice to see you again, Miss Laura. I'll leave you with Mrs Leybourne and go and see that your room's all right. We've put you in your own small room until Mr Christopher comes home.'

She left the kitchen, giving Laura the chance to speak quietly to Jocelyn on her own. 'Jocelyn,' she said, feeling rather shy, 'are you sure you want me here? Isn't it going to make things more difficult for you?' Then she felt her hand taken in a grasp which seemed almost urgent.

'I do want you, Laura. Perhaps I'm a selfish old lady, but I'm on my own all day, except for Mrs Maw and Marcia—well, I have to be honest, Marcia isn't here very often, she seems to spend most of her time over at the farm with Ronald Hobbs. I think you know that it is not one of the Hayle farms.'

'Do you mean . . . ?'

'No, I shouldn't say things like that. But I think that Marcia misses Nicholas and Ronald has been a good friend to her; he is a widower, older than she is, but his children have left home so I think he's glad of her company. I am not saying that there is anything more to it than that.'

Laura was left thinking of the things Nicholas had said that had implied that his marriage wasn't a happy one; here was further evidence, but she made up her mind to try and ignore the situation and to make up to Jocelyn for some of her loneliness.

'It is very kind of you to have me,' she said, and tried to change the subject. 'Mother and Father live in a lovely little cottage, but there wasn't really room for me and a child in the offing.'

'You are pleased, Laura? About the baby, I mean.'

'Yes, I am very pleased,' Laura replied.

'I'm sorry that you were ill in Africa and was glad when that kind doctor insisted on sending you home. It is obvious that hot climates don't suit you. I hope you are not going to find it too cold here at Hayle.'

Laura smiled. 'No, it will be lovely and I am very fit now, you know; I will help you all I can.'

'Thank you, my dear; I must say that you are looking well and the country air will do you good. Now, I must take you up to your room; we've had a hot-water bottle in the bed ever since we received your letter.' Jocelyn made her way out of the kitchen, and Laura followed her up the narrow back stairs which had at one time been the servants' staircase.

'How long has Nicholas got this time?' she asked as they reached the top landing.

'Forty-eight hours; he came this morning. He thinks he will be sent out east now that it's all flaring up over there. What a dreadful war it is; hardly any part of the world that is not involved and no end in sight. We might be out of it here in Richmond, but there are constant reminders, especially with Nicholas and Christopher being away.'

'You've not heard from Christopher?'

'Not a word, you know what it was like last time. If only we knew where he was, we could let him know about the baby.' As they got to the bedroom door, Jocelyn turned and took Laura's arm. 'I'm so excited to think I am going to be a grandmother; bless you, my dear.'

In spite of the strained atmosphere between Marcia and Jocelyn, Laura was happy to be back at Hayle. She unpacked her suitcase and, looking out of the window, she had a last glimpse of the garden and the trees, black in their winter bareness as the light faded; then she had to pull the curtains.

At dinner that night, Marcia seemed more amiable and it was a pleasant meal, Nicholas being in very good spirits, away for a few hours from his nights in the air.

Laura slept well and late, but she did not think it would matter. She wondered if Marcia was going to the farm and, if so, would she, Laura, see anything of Nicholas? She longed to be with him yet felt frightened of her own emotions. She had become used to thinking of the coming child as Christopher's, but now with Nicholas so near, she began to wonder how in the future she would ever be able to forget that the child was his. It was a worrying, fearsome thought, so much so that she did her best to bury it deep in her subconscious mind. Once Christopher is here, she assured herself, it will be different.

She got downstairs to find that everyone had finished breakfast, but Mrs Maw gladly made her tea and toast and she took it through into the drawing-room where Nicholas and his mother were sitting deep in conversation and where already there was a fire blazing.

Laura greeted them and asked if Marcia had gone to the farm.

Nicholas replied and Laura thought that his voice held a note of amusement. 'Yes, she says that Ronald couldn't spare her; I think she helps with the milking. She seems to love it and if you could only imagine how sophisticated Marcia used to be, you would hardly credit the change in her or how anyone could have taken to farming as happily as she has. War makes strange creatures of us; I used to be a sober solicitor and now I'm supposed to be an air ace.'

'What are you going to do this morning, Nicholas?' his mother asked. 'You don't have to go back until this evening, do you?'

Nicholas did not reply immediately and looked at Laura. 'Feel like coming for a walk, Laura, down to the wood and back? It's a cold morning, but it's fine and dry.'

'Don't you have business to see to, Nicholas?' Laura asked. 'There must be a lot of things your father would have done.'

He grinned. 'We are lucky in having a good friend of Father's who is not long retired; he promised to keep an eye on things until I return. Mother does her bit, as well. I saw to everything which was necessary yesterday so I have a free morning.' He turned to Jocelyn. 'Mother, you don't mind if I take Laura off, do you? You'll have her all to yourself for months and months.'

Jocelyn laughed. 'I am only too pleased that you are getting on well together; off you go while you've got the chance. But wrap up well, Laura.'

Laura couldn't say no and went off to put on an extra cardigan underneath her coat, she also wore a bright red woollen headscarf which Nicholas admired, saying it looked cheerful.

They walked briskly and he took her hand. The lawns and gardens looked flat and lifeless until they got to the edge of the shrubbery where Laura found a lovely clump of snowdrops.

She stood looking at them. 'In the midst of everything which seems dead and dormant, you suddenly find beauty. I think it teaches us that even in the blackest times, there is always something good to be found.'

'I think we shall find some more growing in the wood,' said Nicholas, looking at the girl at his side who was beautiful herself with the glowing good looks of someone enjoying the promise of new life.

Although the day was cold, they sat on the seat as they had done before.

'It may be a long time before I am here again,' said Nicholas. 'Goodness knows where I'm going to get a posting, though I've a feeling it will be out east; the Air Force is playing a big part in the Burma campaign.' His thoughts seemed to project into the future.

'But you'll be here when I come back; that's a nice thought, Laura.'

She looked up at him. 'I don't know if I shall be at Hayle,' she replied. 'Christopher might want to live in Richmond and I don't want to encroach on Marcia.'

'Damn, Marcia.' His words were explosive and Laura felt uncomfortable. 'She does her best to make Mother feel unwanted, and I shall be furious if she takes the same attitude with you. I am glad that you are here, Laura; I am glad to be able to go off and know that Mother will have you. She is so looking forward to having a grandchild.'

His words reminded Laura of his expression when they had all stood together in the hall on her arrival the day before. 'But, Nicholas, you are not at all pleased; why did you look so put out when it was mentioned by Marcia?'

For reply, he put a hand on each of her shoulders and drew her close to him; then his fingers tilted her chin to look at him and he met her eyes unflinchingly.

'Laura, I am jealous. Jealous of my own brother. I wish the child could have been mine.'

Inwardly, Laura flinched; she went cold, unable to find words. Her instinct was to throw herself into his arms and tell him the truth, but something stopped her. Everyone was so pleased because it was Christopher's child; the complications of letting the true facts be

196

known were insuperable. She sat stiff and sick, conscious of the lie she had begun and must continue; conscious of this man whom for one night she had loved and who was now sitting so neat to her.

He did not seem to notice her silence.

'I am sorry, Laura, I have shocked you. I shouldn't have said that or felt like that; it was just a gut reaction and shows just how much I feel for you. I suppose if things had been better between Marcia and myself and if we'd had the family I wanted, then I wouldn't have reacted in that way. Don't take any notice of me; I just hope that you will be very happy here at Hayle with my mother, and that the baby will be born safely and give you much joy. Now, let us talk of happier things, not my mixed-up emotions. You know I have come home on leave especially to see you, Laura?'

'Nicholas.' He had succeeded in breaking her taut spell by saying something completely outrageous.

'Mother wrote and told me that you were coming and I asked for leave. I wanted to see you so much, Laura. I've not forgotten the last time we met, you know.'

'Nicholas, we *must* forget it,' she said nervously.

'I know, I know, but it gives me great joy to think of you as you were that night and I was determined to see you once more before I was sent abroad. You can't deny that you were pleased to see me when you arrived.' He started to laugh and she joined in.

'Yes, I was, Nicholas; it was so unexpected and Marcia was so shocked, but you were very naughty to kiss me like that.'

'I would like to more than kiss you, Laura.'

'Nicholas, you keep saying the most shocking things, and it is getting cold sitting here; I think it's about time we made our way back to the house.' Laura started to get up, but he drew her back.

'Just one more minute; I will keep you warm.' And he slid his arms underneath her thick coat and pulled her very close; she felt his lips on hers for long precious moments.

'You are more beautiful than ever, my Laura,' he whispered. 'I know you are not my Laura, but just for these few moments, I want to claim you, for things will never be the same again. When I return—I suppose I should say if I return—you will be settled down with Christopher and I must try to make a go of things with Marcia.'

Laura was silent as she looked across the dale from the shelter of the trees. The moor was brown with dead heather and bracken; in the distance the hills were a blue-grey in the winter mist. She would be able to come to this spot when she wanted quiet and solitude, but she would always remember Nicholas when she was here.

She looked at him. 'I expect it has been

difficult for Marcia, with you not being here,' she said quietly. 'I am sure that it will be different once the war is over and things get back to normal. We just have to hope and pray that we won't be invaded.'

'Thank you, Laura, for saying that,' he murmured. 'And of course, you are quite right. I shall remember your words when I am in some god-forsaken place, and I shall think of you all the time. We must go back to Mother now; it's not fair to leave her on her own when it's my last morning.'

No more was said between them as they walked quietly back to the house and Laura was not to see Nicholas on his own again. She and Jocelyn stood on the steps and waved goodbye as Joe drove off and Laura knew that it was a sad moment not only for her mother-in-law, but also for herself.

Jocelyn voiced her feelings as they turned back into the house. 'Both Nicholas and Christopher away fighting now; it's not much fun being a mother with two sons in a war, Laura, but I mustn't grumble, and I pray that they will come back safely. I am very glad that you are here.'

Winter soon turned to spring and Laura felt well and happy. There was an uneasy truce with Marcia, but she did not see a lot of her sister-in-law, who seemed to spend more time than ever at the farm.

Laura had met Ronald Hobbs and had liked

him. He was a quiet, unassuming man, who must have been about fifty years of age; his hair was still dark with no signs of grey. He had the weather-beaten complexion of the farmer and Laura sensed that his relationship with Marcia was a very comfortable and easy one, though he did seem to be the last type of person to whom the sophisticated Marcia would have turned. But Laura could not imagine that there was anything in the friendship which would jeopardize Marcia's marriage, and she believed she had been right in saying to Nicholas that all would be well once the war was over.

In Jocelyn, Laura found a good friend in spite of the differences in their ages; they shared the work of keeping the house in order and, as Marcia had made no changes in the household and kept herself in the big flat, their tasks were not too difficult. The family had been told at the beginning of the war that they must be prepared to take in soldiers or evacuees but, as none appeared, they thought they were too isolated for anyone to be conveniently placed there. The house was not big enough to take a whole school, so farms and family were left in peace to do what they could with the land.

Time seemed to pass slowly for Laura, though in a sense life was not unpleasant. The worst thing was the lack of news from either Nicholas or Christopher; the war news was not good, either. It was the middle of 1942, with Rommel on the offensive in North Africa and the Japanese victorious in the Far East; only from Russia was there any encouraging news, after the Germans had suffered defeat in the severe winter.

Then suddenly, and within two days, Jocelyn had word from both Nicholas and Christopher.

The postman had arrived on his bicycle from Richmond in the middle of the morning and Jocelyn excitedly went in search of Laura. She found her daughter-in-law struggling with her bulky figure and the weeds in the border of the back garden.

'Laura, Laura, come quickly.'

Laura looked up and could see from Jocelyn's face that it was not bad news; she hurried back to the house.

'There's a letter from Nicholas; not much news, but he's well and he's in India. He sends you his love and to Marcia.' Jocelyn stopped and looked at Laura in dismay. 'Oh dear, that makes it sound as though he hasn't written to Marcia, doesn't it? I hope she won't be cross. But we've got his address now and I'll be able to write to him; he'll want to know how you are.'

Laura gave Jocelyn a kiss. 'I'm so pleased. I'll walk over to the farm and tell Marcia, if you like.'

'Would you, dear? That would be very kind of you.'

Laura could sense the unspoken feelings and it was why she had made the offer; she knew that Marcia was capable of being scathing about Jocelyn receiving the letter.

A stony track connected Hayle House to the Hobbs farmhouse, but as Laura walked along it, she knew that it was possible that Marcia might be out in the fields somewhere.

In fact, it was Meg she found first; Laura had renewed her acquaintance with Meg and the two girls were good friends. Meg was now married to Rob, but still living at Clapgate Lodge; she often came over to Hayle to see Laura in the evenings.

Laura found Meg in the hen-house.

'Meg,' she called out. 'Where's Marcia? We've had some news from Nicholas.'

Meg, looking sturdy and tanned, came running across the farmyard.

'Oh, Laura, I'm so pleased. Where is he?'

'India at the moment.'

'He and Rob haven't managed to stay together, then?' said Meg.

Rob was somewhere in the Middle East.

'It doesn't look like it, but where is Marcia? I must tell her.'

Meg pulled a face. 'Do you mean that Nicholas has written to his mother and not to Marcia?'

'Yes.'

Both girls were thinking the same thing, but Meg told Laura that Ronald and Marcia were haymaking in the Long Lane field. Laura knew where it was and set off to walk over the fields. She enjoyed the fresh air and the wide open views towards Marske, and she was not long in fording the haymaking party which consisted of Ronald and Marcia and two of the older village men who had served in the last war and were now too old to fight.

Ronald was the first to spot her and came running over.

'Everything all right, Laura? Not bad news, I hope, to bring you all this way?'

He was smiling broadly at her and she liked the open friendliness of his brown face. He called to Marcia who came hurrying up.

'What on earth brings you here, Laura? Are you all right?'

Laura nodded. 'Jocelyn has received a letter from Nicholas; we thought you'd like to know. He's in India.'

Marcia didn't sound pleased. 'Do you mean that he's written to his mother and not to me? Typical of Nicholas.'

'I expect there's a letter for you on the way, Marcia.' Laura tried to sound tactful.

'Don't you believe it. He knows I wouldn't write to him and he can rely on hearing from his dear mother.' She saw Laura's look of dismay and explained resentfully. 'We quarrelled on his last leave, if you must know. I didn't expect him to write to me.'

'I'm sorry, Marcia.' Laura felt awkward

standing there in the hayfield, with Marcia's words spoiling what should have been a happy occasion in a lovely setting.

Then Ronald put an arm round Marcia and, as Laura stood watching them, she saw Marcia kiss his cheek and put her head against his shoulder.

'Never mind, Marcia,' he said with a laugh. 'You've always got me.'

'Thank you, Ronald,' Marcia replied with a smile. 'We'd better get back to the haymaking. Thank you for coming, Laura, but it could have waited until tonight.'

Laura turned away, frustrated and angry. What was Marcia up to, behaving with Ronald like that, and so openly?

Then, as she reached the gate, she was overcome by misgivings and shame. How can I judge her, she said to herself? I made love with her husband and I'm expecting his child; I cannot condemn Marcia for being offhand about him and making up to another man. It's one big muddle, she thought, and I'm not going to make it any better by thinking badly of Marcia. She walked slowly back to Hayle, her excitement and pleasure spoiled, though she must try not to communicate her feelings to Jocelyn.

Two days later, the postman brought another letter, this time from Christopher.

Jocelyn opened the envelope and handed the letter over to Laura; she had tears in her eyes.

Laura took it and read the words aloud.

On leave in Cairo for a week. Hope
you are well. Give my love to Laura
when she gets back. Love Christopher.

Jocelyn was laughing delightedly. 'Oh, isn't
that just like him? No address to write to, but
at least we know he is well and where he is.'

'And to think we've heard from them both in
the same week,' said Laura. 'Oh, I wish the
war was over and that they were safely home.'

'Don't upset yourself, my dear; just to have
heard from them seems to give hope, doesn't
it?'

*   *   *

It was about this time that Laura had an
argument with Dr Ross, who came out to see
her from Richmond. She knew she was to
blame, because she had lied to him about the
date of her last period so that the expected
delivery date of the baby would fit in with
Christopher's last visit home. Dr Ross told her
bluntly that he didn't agree with her and was
she sure she had got her dates right. She knew
she would have to go on lying and let it be
thought that the baby had arrived a month
early.

They had arranged for a midwife to come

out from Richmond for a few days, and when Laura knew that it was time to phone her in the middle of June and a month early, she put everyone in a panic. But Nurse Willox arrived, Laura gave birth easily, and within hours she was holding her baby son in her arms.

Her emotions on looking at the baby were so complex that she was overwhelmed. Fortunately, Nurse Willox, a sensible and kindly Scottish girl, was used to weepy mothers, especially the ones whose husbands were away from home, and she left Laura quietly to her own thoughts.

Laura's mind was in chaos; it was as though she had got the two brothers muddled up. Christopher will be thrilled, she found herself saying, and then cried out loudly from the depths of her heart. Nicholas, Nicholas, this little boy is yours and you will never know. A great sense of wickedness at denying Nicholas his own child forced her to lie back on the pillows and sob.

At that moment, the nurse brought Jocelyn into the room.

'Laura, Laura,' came the whisper. 'Don't cry. Are you all right? Nurse says that it's a boy, what wonderful news! Can I see him, will you let me hold him for a moment?'

Laura sat up weakly and smiled at her mother-in-law. The baby was cradled in older arms and Laura saw the tears running down Jocelyn's cheeks.

Then Jocelyn gave a gasp as she pulled back the shawl and saw the baby's face for the first time.

'Laura,' she cried, as though stupefied. 'Laura, he's the image of Nicholas. He's just like Nicholas when he was born, I shall never forget.'

This innocent remark, so full of pleasure, nearly finished Laura and seemed to stab her in the heart; for it was true, the baby had a lot of dark hair and not the fair hair of Christopher, and his eyes were dark, too. She struggled with her tears, with her feelings and her sense of guilt, then from her lips came bright and sensible words which made her shudder.

'Yes, he is, isn't he? But my father has got brown hair and eyes, too, so it's on both sides of the family and not so surprising.'

Meg came to see her that evening, and the next day, Marcia came with Ronald at her side; the congratulations were polite from Marcia and enthusiastic and kindly from Ronald.

Laura decided to call her baby Jonathan Robert; Jocelyn approved of the choice of names and was delighted with the Robert. When Laura saw the father's name on the birth certificate, she panicked for a moment. Have I commited perjury, she thought, is it a crime? Then she took a deep breath and told herself that no one would ever know and the surname was correct after all; Jonathan *was* a

Leybourne.

In July, when Jonathan was a month old, Jocelyn made Laura invite her parents over for a few days. Laura was pleased, for she had been feeling sad that they seemed to be left out, although they did correspond regularly.

When the day of the visit came, her mother was thrilled with the baby and was convinced that he was just like Laura's father; this remark amused Laura, and it was rather a comfort to her. They stayed three days, got on very well with Jocelyn, and loved Hayle House and the surrounding countryside.

Laura was keen to have Jonathan christened, but was hesitating because she did not know who to ask for godparents, being reluctant to ask Marcia who did not like children and had little time for the fuss being made over the new baby.

Then, in the middle of August, there was an unexpected homecoming. Laura had just settled Jonathan in his Moses basket—saved for all those years by Jocelyn—when Meg came running in; she was very excited.

'Laura, I've had a phone call from Rob; he's in London and is coming up first thing tomorrow. He's got ten days before going out East.'

Laura gave the girl a hug. 'I'm so pleased, Meg, that's wonderful news.' Then she had a thought. 'Meg, do you suppose . . . do you think that while Rob is here, you and he could

208

be godparents to Jonathan? I want to have him christened, but I haven't known whom I could ask.'

Meg nodded enthusiastically. 'Laura, it's lovely of you to ask us; I am very honoured and I'm sure Rob will be, too. We'll come over and see you tomorrow evening.'

The day of the christening arrived, fortunately fine, for they had to walk down into Marske, even though it meant a long climb up the hill on the way home. All went well; there were celebrations and champagne when they got back to Hayle House and much laughter when Jocelyn remarked that it must be the first time ever that a member of the Leybourne family had been walked to his christening.

The happy weekend over, they all got back to the business of keeping house, farming, and in the evenings listening to the news on the wireless and being cheered by Tommy Handley in 'ITMA' and Jack Warner in 'Garrison Theatre'.

It was at about this time that changes were taking place in the North African campaign and Lieutenant-General Montgomery was put in charge of the Eighth Army. Both Laura and Jocelyn listened to every news bulletin, knowing that Christopher must be amongst the fighting force; cheers went up whenever Rommel retreated.

Laura felt happy that autumn; it was a

season she loved in any case and it gave her a great deal of pleasure to wheel Jonathan down to the wood, even though the last part of the walk was rather bumpy. Then she would sit on the seat with him on her lap and think of Nicholas and Christopher, and imagine in the sunshine that she could see the leaves changing colour.

The leaves were golden when the news of the battle of El Alamein came through. Casualties were high, but Laura thought of Christopher as a survivor and when the notification came from the War Office, she held the piece of paper with a cold numbness of disbelief and shock.

Leybourne, Christopher Robert, Captain
Missing believed dead.

That was all.

CHAPTER NINE

Laura clutched the piece of paper. She felt no emotion except an enormous sense of pity, not for herself, but for Jocelyn; it was as though she could not think of herself for Jocelyn's loss seemed so much greater. First Robert, now Christopher. How was she going to tell her?

'Laura.'

Jocelyn had come up quietly from the direction of the kitchen and Laura, standing stunned by the front door, did not hear her.

'Laura, what is it? You are white. What are you holding? Is it the post?'

'Oh, Jocelyn.'

Laura put an arm round her mother-in-law as though she was trying to shield her from the terrible news.

'Is it Christopher or Nicholas?'

'Jocelyn, it's Christopher. Oh, I'm sorry, I'm so sorry.'

Jocelyn took the short letter and read it. She seemed dazed.

Then she said, 'I must show it to Bates, he will know what it means.'

Laura looked at the older woman with immense pity; had she taken in the dreadful words? But Jocelyn had turned and hurried over to the coach-house to find Bates. He had lived over the coach-house all the years he had been at Hayle and although he was now over seventy, he still served the family and Jocelyn had let him stay there.

On her own, Laura tried to gather up her thoughts. Christopher, oh Christopher. She cried out his name and found to her horror that she could hardly remember him. It's the shock, she told herself; we'd better have some tea or some brandy. I'll go and tell Mrs Maw. She will be upset, too.

By the time she had reached the kitchen,

211

Jocelyn came rushing back accompanied by Bates. The old man went straight up to Laura.

'Miss Laura,' he said, and his voice wavered, 'it doesn't mean Mr Christopher has been killed; he might have been taken prisoner. I've told Mrs Leybourne. You must have hope; the War Office will keep you informed. I was a prisoner in 1918 and I was reported missing, but I came home all right after the war. You mustn't give up hope, Miss Laura.'

Laura took his hand and smiled. 'Thank you, Bates, you are very kind; it's a help to us all to have you here.'

Jocelyn was clinging to Mrs Maw and both of them were crying; Laura did not say anything, but put the kettle on and made tea, then she went through to the dining-room to fetch the brandy.

She was aware of a terrible remote feeling as though it wasn't happening to her, as if Christopher belonged to his mother and to Bates and Mrs Maw, but not to her. She put her hands on Jocelyn's arm. 'Do you mind if I walk down to the wood? I want to be on my own. But I won't stay there long; you'll be all right with Mrs Maw, won't you?'

'I understand, Laura, I understand; you need to be on your own.'

Mrs Maw put an arm around Jocelyn while Laura hurried to fetch her coat and scarf.

Without thought of having made any movement, she found herself sitting on the

212

seat, but it was not of Christopher she thought—it was of Nicholas. 'Oh, what is wrong with me?' she cried out. 'Nicholas, I want you here, I want to feel your arms about me. No, that is wrong of me, I must think, I must think.'

And she tried to think of Christopher. Her most vivid recollection of him was when they had jumped into the sea together at Dunkirk and he had held her up.

What else, what else? Those nice days at Marlow, a brief wedding, a farewell and two days here in Swaledale. Four days I knew him, and now it is as though I never knew him. He has gone and he was never here. I was fond of him, I was very fond of him, but how can I say that I shall ever miss him? And how can I tell Jocelyn all this? I can never explain. She has lost the dear son she knew for twenty-five years; she knew him as a baby, as a child, as a young man: she has lost everything unless what Bates says is true. I must try and comfort her and give her hope.

And for myself, no one will ever understand that I do not know what I have lost; I have Jonathan and he will be my life. And she suddenly remembered him asleep in his cot, possibly awake and crying for her.

'I'm a fool,' she said, 'a wicked fool,' and she got up and ran all the way back to the house to arrive panting in the hall to find Jocelyn coming down the stairs with a smiling child in her arms.

Miraculously, Jocelyn was smiling, too. 'It may not be the end of the world,' she said to Laura. 'And we must make the most of Jonathan. What a blessing he will be to you, Laura; I am very sorry, my dear. I thought only of my own loss, and it's far worse for you because you are so young with your life only just beginning. Will you forgive me?'

They hugged each other and Laura took the baby and held him close. 'There's nothing to forgive. I was thinking that it's far worse for you because you have lost your baby as well as your son. We must talk about him, Jocelyn; you must show me the old photographs and tell me your memories of him. It will help us both.'

'I will write to Nicholas,' said Jocelyn. 'I wish he was here.'

'Yes, we must think of Nicholas. When he comes home, he and Marcia may have a family and it will make up to you for losing Christopher.'

Jocelyn nodded, but the shake of her head was thoughtful and somewhat dubious. 'I cannot imagine Nicholas and Marcia as parents, but perhaps I am looking on the black side. We are living in the lap of the gods in this war; we must hope and pray that Christopher will be returned to us and that Nicholas will come through it all safely, too.'

Laura put an arm round her. 'Jocelyn, you

are brave and sensible and I must try to be more like you; I am so glad that I am here with you.'

In spite of their words, they were stunned and disbelieving for many days. The loss of human life is one of the facts of war, but when it happens to you, Laura thought, it is as though you are the only one in the world to suffer, whereas all over Britain, there will be wives and mothers receiving letters and telegrams containing news which will change their lives and bring them heartache and sadness.

That winter was a sober time for those living at Hayle House; it was only the sight of Jonathan growing into a sturdy little boy which brought them any pleasure at all. Marcia spent more and more time at the farm and Laura noticed that often she did not come home at night.

Laura loved her little boy and was happy to be at Hayle with Jocelyn, but as the months passed by and the war progressed, she began to have feelings of uselessness. She was fit and well and full of energy and she found, to her dismay, that it did not satisfy her to be at home looking after a young child when she could have been using her skills at a military hospital or rehabilitation centre. She said nothing of these thoughts to Jocelyn and had no idea that her feelings were showing on her face until, one day very near to Jonathan's first birthday, her mother-in-law had a long talk with her.

It was June of 1943; the most encouraging news on the war front was the collapse of the Axis powers in Tunisia and the subsequent Allied landing in Sicily; fighting continued on the Russian front, and the news from India and Burma was spasmodic. Jocelyn received the occasional letter from Nicholas, still in India, but these said little except that he was well. Reading between the lines, they could sense his longing to be back at Hayle.

But at Hayle, the war seemed remote and this served only to add to Laura's sense of futility; she was torn in two, content with the country lifestyle, but frustrated at not being able to play the part she had chosen at the outbreak of the war. At the same time, she felt a sense of shame that she could be so dissatisfied, and unknown to herself she had become quiet and withdrawn.

Jocelyn tackled her about it one day when they were wheeling Jonathan in his push-chair through the garden. They were making for the wood with the intention of enjoying an hour's sunshine on the seat under the trees.

Laura said very little as they walked along; Jocelyn was pushing Jonathan as she always loved to do, and it was not until they reached the wooden seat and sat down that anything was said. All was quiet around them except for the bird-song and the softest rustle of the leaves as a light breeze blew through the trees;

Jonathan had fallen asleep or the air would have been filled with his happy laugh.

Jocelyn spoke suddenly and almost abruptly. 'Are you going to tell me what is wrong, Laura?'

Laura turned her head sharply at the question and looked at the older woman she had come to love.

'Why, Jocelyn, what do you mean? There is nothing wrong; you know that I am very happy here.'

Jocelyn smiled. 'I know you love Hayle and you have Jonathan, but for a little while now I have sensed a restlessness in you. I believe you would like to go back to nursing. Am I right?'

Laura got up in reply and walked along the cliff path. However had Jocelyn guessed her feelings? She thought she had succeeded in hiding how she felt. But she knew that she could be honest with her mother-in-law and perhaps it would do her good to talk about it. She returned to the seat.

She took Jocelyn's hand and smiled warmly. 'I can't hide things from you, can I? But it seems wrong of me to feel fed up when I have you and Jonathan and it is so lovely here. Yes, I would like to be nursing again, but I know it is impossible so I must find some patience from somewhere and wait and see what is going to happen; the war can't go on for ever.'

'It is now we have to think about, Laura, not the years to come. Why do you say it is impossible for you to go nursing again—?'

'But, Jocelyn,' Laura interrupted hastily, 'how can I work? I have Jonathan to think of and care for. That should be enough for me.'

'Listen to me, Laura; you are young and fit and the country needs people like you. If you could get a nursing post, I would take care of Jonathan for you. He is a baby no longer; would you trust him to me?'

Laura gazed at the older woman. 'Are you really serious, Jocelyn?' she asked.

'Of course I am, and I am sure there is nothing unusual in it. There must be young women all over the country in munitions factories, on the farms, doing the work the men would have done, leaving their children with grandmothers and aunts and uncles.'

'I don't know what to say.' Laura felt confused. Jocelyn was offering her a lifeline to get her back to work, but should she take it?

'My dear girl, don't give me a reply now. Think it over; ring up one or two hospitals; there is the garrison at Catterick, they are sure to need trained staff like yourself.'

'Jocelyn, don't go so fast!' Laura found herself laughing. 'You are too good to me, you know. Please don't think I am hesitating because I don't want to leave Jonathan with you. I think it would be lovely for both of you. But you see, all these months I've had this yearning to go back to nursing, and now that you are offering me the chance, I can't believe it's true.'

For the rest of that day, Laura felt a sense of excitement. Jocelyn had mentioned the garrison hospital at Catterick and Laura knew that was where she would like to be. The army garrison was almost part of Richmond, but how would she get there? It would mean buying a car, but would she get a petrol allowance? Ideas teemed through her brain until she knew that she was taking Jocelyn's suggestion seriously. She couldn't wait to get in touch with the hospital; she made up her mind there and then and decided to go and tell Jocelyn.

She found her mother-in-law cleaning silver in the kitchen, and Jocelyn smiled brightly. 'I can tell from your face that you've been thinking about my suggestion. Come and sit down and talk to me, what have you decided?'

Laura was slow to reply. 'Well, I thought I'd made up my mind to go back to nursing, but seeing you so busy has made me realize that I cannot ask you to look after Jonathan and keep this big house going at the same time.'

'That is no problem; you are not to give it a minute's thought,' replied Jocelyn. 'I've thought it over and have made up my mind to have a girl up from the village to help in the house. There is sure to be someone leaving school this term who will be glad of a job; it's not easy for the local girls to get to Richmond to work. Mrs Maw isn't getting any younger and it will be a help to her, too; she is sure to know of someone.'

Laura kissed her. 'You are a darling. If you are quite certain that Jonathan will not be too much for you, I'd love to try and get into the hospital at Catterick. I'm used to nursing soldiers and although it might be hard work, they are great fun to be with. I shall have to try and get a lift into Richmond, then I will go out to the hospital to see Matron.'

'Why don't you ring her up?' Jocelyn asked.

'Shall I?'

'Yes, do it straight away; there's no sense in losing any time now that you've made up your mind.'

Minutes later, Laura was talking to the matron of the garrison hospital.

'QA?' said a deep, brisk voice at the other end of a poor line.

'Yes, I was in France and North Africa, but came home because I was pregnant. Now my mother-in-law says that she will look after my little boy so I am free to work again.'

'Splendid. We've just lost Sister in the surgical ward. Can you start straight away?'

Laura felt her breath taken away. 'Well, yes, but I've got to get some transport first. Do you know if I'll get a petrol allowance?'

'No problem; get yourself a car, come and see me and I'll arrange it for you. Come as soon as you can, we're desperate.'

Laura put down the receiver feeling that her

life had been changed in the space of a short telephone call. No turning back, she thought; I'll have to see if I can get a lift into Richmond to see about a car.

Getting into Richmond had been one of the biggest problems of the war for those living in the surrounding villages and they had all felt it at Hayle; the Leybournes' old Wolseley was laid up in the garage and they had to rely on lifts with Ronald or Marcia who went into the town once a week on farm business.

So Laura told a very pleased Jocelyn the outcome of the conversation with Matron and said that she would take Jonathan over to the farm when he woke up to see if she could beg a lift.

The farmhouse at Hobbs farm was a long, low rambling building of mellowed stone which had withstood centuries of rough weather on the cliff edge. Laura did not know where to look for Ronald, but was fortunate enough to find Marcia in the large kitchen. As usual, it was a Marcia who was cheerful when away from Hayle House and she greeted Laura happily, but totally ignored Jonathan.

'This is nice, Laura; we don't often see you here. Have you come for a lift into Richmond? I think Ronald is going tomorrow afternoon.'

'I've got to get to Catterick somehow,' replied Laura, and explained what she was going to do.

'Well done, you.' Marcia was enthusiastic.

'I'd go mad stuck at home all day.'

'I shall have to get a car, Marcia; I'm going to see if Joe Sleightholme knows of one for sale. I can get a petrol allowance.'

Marcia was thoughtful, then she spoke quickly. 'But, Laura, you don't have to buy one. You can borrow mine. Didn't you know I had a car? It's a little Austin and has been stuck in the stables at Hayle ever since the war started; Bates has kept an eye on it for me. I'd be only too pleased to have it used.'

'Are you sure, Marcia?'

'Yes, certain; I'll get Ronald to come over with a can of petrol tonight and get it going for you. No, it's no trouble. I'm pleased to help and I'm pleased you're going back to nursing. We've all got to help, haven't we?'

Laura had not found Marcia so talkative for a long time. They had tea together, then Marcia suddenly became quite friendly. She showed Jonathan the ducks and geese in the farmyard and gave him some bread to throw for them. Laura looked on in astonishment, for Marcia had always ignored Jonathan completely.

Ronald got the car going that night and Laura was thrilled with it; she went up and down the drive at Hayle several times and soon got used to it.

At the garrison hospital the next day, she had her interview with Matron and agreed to start the following day. She felt proud to be in

222

her grey dress and scarlet cape once again and it helped to dispel the feeling of nervousness as she reported for duty on the ward.

Laura had precisely two minutes in which to feel nervous, for immediately she had to take the night sister's report and was whisked into a round of familiar duties which did not end until five o'clock. They were desperately short staffed, but she soon found that the more mobile of the patients willingly helped with dishing-up meals and other such duties.

On that first day, it took her only half an hour to realize that she had done the right thing and she knew that she was where she wanted to be. She hardly stopped for lunch, as they were preparing for the surgeon's round—wartime didn't alter the strict rules which surrounded his visit.

When Laura saw a tall man standing in the office, she knew that Mr Greenway had arrived and she hurried in to introduce herself. Words almost failed her when she saw him, for had he been a little younger and in an air force uniform, she would have mistaken him for Nicholas. The likeness was uncanny; the same dark hair and eyes, the same rather stern expression which she remembered from her first meeting with Nicholas. It was only as she shook hands with him and spoke to him that she realized that he must be in his fifties, twenty years older than Nicholas.

'Sister Leybourne, from what Matron has

told me, your phone call saved the day. Sister Bridgman was called away to be posted to the Far East and we were already short staffed. I am very pleased to meet you and have you here.'

Although she was bemused by his astonishing likeness to Nicholas, she managed to say the right things and accompanied him on his round. She knew that miracles of surgery had been performed on shattered limbs; James Greenway remembered every patient's name and he was obviously well liked. But she found herself giving a sigh of relief as he left the ward, for her initial shock on seeing him had made her realize how vulnerable her feelings were. She needed a busy spell on the ward to harden her up, she said to herself.

The little car seemed to take only minutes to get back to Hayle, and soon after five o'clock she was hugging Jonathan and laughing with Jocelyn; both of them had a lot to talk about.

Mrs Maw had found a girl who was due to leave school at the end of term, but the headmistress was willing to let her go early to work at Hayle House. In fact, Marjorie Barstow came along to see them that very evening and started work the next day.

By the new year of 1944, Laura felt as though she had never worked anywhere else but the army hospital at Catterick and she had never known time to pass so quickly. Jonathan had not suffered in any way by the separation from his mother and Laura looked forward each day to the hour of bath and bedtime. Jonathan loved his grandmother and indeed his very first word had been 'Nana' and not 'Mummy'.

Days off were taken up with recuperating for the next spell of work and Laura certainly did not have the time to grieve over Christopher or to think about Nicholas.

At the hospital, she came to know and like and respect Mr Greenway and he soon insisted that she call him James; in many ways, he reminded her of Dr Kinghorn and Dr Neale and Dr Franks, and she found herself amused that she had made good friends of all her superior officers.

It was when Laura went on to a period of night duty as the year came up to Christmas that she had the opportunity of getting to know him much better. She wondered if he ever took any time off to rest, for whenever she seemed to be on duty, he would be busy in the operating theatre and often called back for emergencies. He lived in a small town house in Richmond.

One evening on the ward, when she had settled a young soldier who had had a foot amputated and had left a nurse to sit by his bed, she returned to her office to find Mr Greenway sitting there, still in his green theatre gown and holding his cap in motionless fingers. His very stillness was an indication of his tiredness, for his personality was a lively one and he always seemed to be active and on the move.

She sat across the small table from him and slowly he lifted his face to hers; their eyes met and a wave of sympathy passed between them.

'James.' Laura's voice was quiet. 'You have been operating all day, can't you go home now and get some rest?'

'I could,' he replied, 'but I don't want to.'

She looked up in surprise, wondering what he meant, but he went on speaking as though she was not there.

'I don't think I can face my thoughts on my own tonight. So many tragedies today; one boy we've lost and now this one without a foot. Is the war never going to end, Laura? Surely with the Americans behind us, we could attack the bloody Germans across the Channel and put an end to it all? But even when that's over, there's the Japanese though I must say that the news from there has been a bit better; some of these boys have been in Burma, you know.'

She nodded. 'Yes, I know, I've been talking to them. My brother-in-law is out there somewhere and we haven't heard from him for a long time now. We dread to hear from the War Office.'

He looked at her. 'Can I stay and talk to you for a little while, Laura? You are the only sane thing in this war.' He grinned suddenly. 'That

226

doesn't sound very complimentary, does it, but I value these moments. Can you get us some coffee? You need a break, too, you've got the whole night in front of you.'

She put the kettle on and then helped him out of his gown and put it in the laundry basket. She glanced into the ward and saw that all was quiet, so she quickly made two mugs of coffee and found a tin of biscuits.

'Biscuits, Laura? Is this your ration? I can't deprive you.'

'I don't eat many,' she laughed. 'I keep them for emergencies and I think this is one. You need the sugar, James.'

'Practical Laura. Tell me about your brother-in-law.'

'His father died two years ago and he's now the owner of the Hayle estate; he has an old family friend to look after it, but I don't think he can wait for the day to come to be back in Yorkshire.'

'And your Christopher, Laura? Still no news?'

'No, nothing. There are times I wonder if I ever married him, it was all so fleeting.' Words seemed to slip out easily to James.

'But you have Jonathan to remind you; he must be a great joy to you.'

Laura swallowed hard; the deceit goes on, she thought. 'Yes, he's wonderful, he's just begun to talk and he's so amusing. But you don't want to hear all this, James.'

She found her hand clasped in a tight grip, she thought it felt desperate; she looked up and met imploring eyes.

'But I do, Laura, I would talk to you about anything just to take my mind off things and to be with you.'

Quickly she pulled her hand away. 'That is not what I want to hear in Sister's office, James,' she said stiffly.

'I'm so sorry, Laura, I'm just so tired. But the coffee and the short chat are doing the trick—and the biscuits, of course! I'll go home now and try to get some sleep. Pray that we don't get another emergency tonight.' He stood up and then bent over and kissed her quickly on the forehead. 'Thank you, my dear, for being you and for being here. I will see you tomorrow night.'

He left then and Laura sat still for a long time. She liked and respected him so much and did not want emotions spoiling a good friendship and a good working relationship. He needed sleep badly and she was glad for his sake that they were not disturbed that night.

The Christmas holiday coincided with Laura's few days off as she changed from night duty back on to days, and she was glad of the break and the opportunity of spending Christmas with Jonathan.

As she had supper with Jocelyn before going on nights for the last time, she ventured to mention James.

'Jocelyn, I want to ask you something, but I feel a bit reluctant in these days of rationing.'

'My dear Laura, do you want to have a Christmas party or something?'

Laura laughed. 'No, it's not as bad as that. You've heard me speak of James Greenway, the surgeon at the hospital, the one I think looks like Nicholas. Well, I think he is going to be on his own on Christmas Day though he might be on call; I wondered if we could invite him here for Christmas dinner. Would you mind?'

'I'd be delighted, Laura. Ronald has got a turkey for us and I'm sure that Bates could easily produce some extra vegetables. It's no problem at all. We've got plenty of wine which Robert laid down, so why don't we make a celebration of it? It will do us good to have a man about! You ask him, my dear, and I hope he says yes.'

James did say yes. Laura asked him that evening and he seemed delighted, though he admitted that it had been his intention to sleep the clock round on Christmas Day to try and catch up on some rest.

On Christmas Eve, Ronald took them all into Richmond to make last-minute purchases. Laura found a pull-along wooden train for Jonathan, but had difficulty in thinking of something for James; she ended up in the bookshop and bought him Pontefract and Hartley's little book on Swaledale.

On Christmas morning, they all walked down to the church in Marske, and if Jonathan was noisy in the wrong places, nobody seemed to mind very much.

The turkey had been cooking while they were out, and promptly at twelve o'clock James arrived; it was the first time that Laura had seen him out of his hospital clothes and he looked so handsome it gave her quite a shock. She introduced him to Jocelyn and, to her amusement, found them gazing at each other, Jocelyn with a pretty flush on her face.

'You remind me of my elder son,' Laura could hear Jocelyn saying. 'I am so glad that you could come today.'

Then she saw James kiss Jocelyn's cheek to wish her a Happy Christmas before he turned round and picked up Jonathan, whirling him round to shrieks of laughter from the little boy. It became a happy scene and Laura was touched because James had been out and bought them gifts; he produced attractive head-squares for herself and Jocelyn, and a toy car for Jonathan.

Marcia was at the farm with Ronald, but Jocelyn insisted that Mrs Maw and Bates should sit up with them for Christmas dinner, and they all had an enjoyable time.

When they had finished the meal, Laura was wondering if James would go for a walk with her; she felt the need for fresh air and exercise.

But he shook his head with a grin. 'Do you mind if I don't come, Laura? It's my day off and I feel lazy and I don't think we should leave Jocelyn on her own; I'll stay and chat to her if you don't mind going on your own.'

James and Laura had been doing the washing-up at James's insistence, and Jocelyn came into the kitchen at that moment. 'What are you two planning?' she asked.

James put his hand lightly on her shoulder. 'Laura wants me to walk, but I would rather stay and talk to you, Jocelyn.'

She was all smiles, and the two of them turned and went together into the drawing-room.

Laura stared and she, too, smiled. James and Jocelyn, she asked herself? What a lovely idea. They must be about the same age and I can see that they have taken to each other. I will go for a nice long walk and leave them to get to know one another.

She enjoyed her walk and all was well when she returned to the house; Jonathan had woken up happily, and Jocelyn and James were amusing him with his new toys. James had tea before going back to Richmond and they all waved him off from the porch steps.

Jocelyn turned to Laura as they went back into the house. 'Your surgeon is a very nice man, Laura; do invite him to come whenever he feels that he needs a break from the hospital.'

Laura smiled. 'Thank you, Jocelyn, I am very pleased to find that you liked him so much.'

CHAPTER TEN

The first months of the new year of 1944 saw Jocelyn getting more and more worried and morose when there was no news of Nicholas; reports came through of the Burma campaign and they imagined that he must be part of it. Laura was pleased to feel that, during the day, Jocelyn had Jonathan to care for and to think about; he was now well over two years old, strong and active and bursting with energy. Jocelyn found herself glad of Marjorie's help, not only with the household tasks, but also in her willingness to take Jonathan to play outside or to walk down to the farm to feed the ducks and geese.

Laura worked hard at the hospital and so did James; casualties were beginning to trickle in from Italy and, as the fighting seemed to come nearer home, it gave a renewed hope of victory.

But it was not all work, for after the successful Christmas visit, James took to going out to Hayle to see Jocelyn on his free day. Laura was delighted.

The month of June brought joy, hope and

tragedy to Laura all within the space of a few days. She went into the hospital on the morning of 6 June to find all her patients in a buzz of excitement; even the ones who should not have been out of bed were huddled round the wireless, waiting to hear every news bulletin.

By lunchtime, the news was certain and they knew that a landing had been made by British and American troops on the Normandy coast. The Germans were taken by surprise and positions were soon fixed around Caen by the invading troops.

Laura couldn't believe the effect on the morale of her patients; they had waited for it so long and now the excitement was like a current of electricity running through them.

By the time James came running into the ward, Laura was gripped by the same excitement. In front of hooting and whistling young soldiers, he picked her up and swung her round and kissed her.

'James!' she cried out uselessly, against the tumult of noise from the ward, and she could not be cross.

'Laura, it's happened at last. I knew Churchill could do it, and with Eisenhower in command we cannot fail.' He looked around him. 'You won't get your patients away from the wireless for the next few days, but don't let it worry you. They need to heal in mind as well as in body and this is the best medicine we could have given them.'

He made his round and she had never heard him so cheerful and noisy with the young men who were his patients; back in the office, he took her hands in his.

'We are celebrating, Laura, come out to dinner with me tonight.' Then he seemed to turn shy; most unusual in James, thought Laura. 'Do you think Jocelyn would come, too, if I came out to Hayle to fetch you both? Jonathan will be all right with Mrs Maw, won't he? We will go to the King's Head and, God willing, I won't be called out, so we can all walk by the river afterwards. Do you think Jocelyn would like that?'

Laura was laughing at his enthusiasm. 'I'm sure she would love it, James. Shall we be ready for eight o'clock?'

It was a very successful evening and after they had finished a splendid dinner, Jocelyn agreed that it would be nice to walk down to the river. The Swale is wide and boisterous at Richmond, and Laura loved to watch the tumbling waters as they crashed over the stones. Jocelyn was quiet, and Laura noticed that James was holding her hand.

*　　　*　　　*

Laura was always to remember 25 August of that year, 1944. The Germans surrendered in Paris and the event seemed to mark a turning point in the war; at home, she had a dreadful quarrel with Marcia.

Her sister-in-law had spent so much of the summer at the farm that Laura had rarely come into contact with her. She never seemed to know if Marcia had come home to her flat upstairs or had stayed at the farm. When they did meet, Marcia was not unfriendly; she seemed satisfied with her rural life and Laura knew that she worked very hard indeed.

Laura had one free day that week, and although she felt tired, she was determined to make the most of the spell of fine weather. Jonathan, as usual, wanted to feed the ducks and Laura decided that instead of walking down the dry, dusty lane to the farm, they would go the longer way by the fields.

On the way, they had to pass a group of rocks set high above the farm which Jonathan loved to scramble up. Below them, she caught sight of the tractor coming up the rising slope towards the rocks.

Jonathan spotted it, too. 'Ronald!' he called out.

'Yes, Jonathan, he is coming this way; watch the tractor,' said Laura, holding on to the small boy.

But as they watched, the farm vehicle turned and Ronald jumped down; a figure had emerged from a group of trees at the edge of the field. Even from that distance, Laura could see that it was Marcia and then, seconds later, as Ronald reached her, Laura was watching the pair in a passionate embrace. And at that very moment, Jonathan chose to race over the field towards them, shouting at the top of his voice:

'Ronald, Aunty Marcia!'

As Laura watched, the pair jerked apart and Ronald turned to catch up the little boy in his arms as Jonathan reached them. Laura had no choice but to go running after Jonathan, and in her embarrassment she knew she would have to speak to Marcia.

But Marcia behaved as though nothing had happened; she went over to the tractor and swung herself up into the driver's seat.

'Hi, Laura, hello Jonathan, see you later.'

She moved off and Laura was left speaking to Ronald. His face, tanned by his outdoor life, was full of laughter as he spoke to Jonathan, telling the little boy that he would take him to the ducks.

Laura followed with mixed feelings; the embrace had not surprised her, for she had long known of the attachment between Marcia and Ronald, but there had been something open and joyous about it which did not augur well for any future relationship between Marcia and Nicholas. Laura wished that she had not witnessed the scene, and later that day she was not surprised when Marcia brought up the subject.

Her sister-in-law had come home for the

evening meal, which was unusual for her; even more unexpected was Marcia's suggestion that they take a walk down to the wood. Laura set off willingly, but she guessed that Marcia had something in particular to say. She was not wrong.

They were only just out of earshot of the house when Marcia launched her attack. 'Well, Laura, I think I am glad that you saw Ronald kissing me. It gives me a chance to say what I want to say.' Her manner was slightly aggressive and Laura was careful when she replied.

'What do you mean, Marcia? I know that you are very attached to Ronald and that he has been very good to you.'

Marcia smiled with an air of self-satisfaction. 'He's been more than good to me; he is my lover and he has promised that as soon as I can get a divorce from Nicholas, he will marry me.'

'Marcia!'

'You needn't sound shocked.'

Laura was outraged and spoke wrathfully. 'But you can't, Marcia. Nicholas will need you when he comes home, I know he wants a family of his own.'

'Oh, do you, Laura Leybourne, and what do you know about it all? Has Nicholas been complaining about me to you? I thought that he was more than a little fond of you.'

'That's nothing to do with it,' Laura said

hastily and without thought. 'He wants a son, and it's up to you to give him one.'

Laura knew she had said the wrong thing, but even so she was surprised at the venom in Marcia's voice.

'Well, he won't get a son from me and he knows it. I never did intend to have children; Ronald has a grown-up family, he doesn't expect me to have kids.'

'But, Marcia, how can you treat Nicholas like this when he has been away in the war all this time?'

Marcia's voice was full of scorn. 'Listen to Miss Innocent speaking. I suppose you've been faithful to Christopher, but what about that nice surgeon of yours?'

Laura smiled. 'Me and James? No, Marcia, you are quite wrong. Didn't you know that James comes to Hayle to see Jocelyn?'

'Jocelyn?' repeated a startled Marcia. 'My God, I don't believe it. I apologize if I've accused you of being unfaithful, but I want no more said on the subject. I am going to marry Ronald, and that's that.'

But Laura had had enough. 'All I can say is that I'm sorry for Nicholas, sorry for him, do you hear?'

And leaving Marcia where she stood, she ran back to the house and straight up to her room; she flung herself on the bed and cried bitterly. She had no right to condemn Marcia; how could she have spoken like that when there was Jonathan to show for her own infidelity?

But her heart went out to the absent Nicholas, who must have gone through a beastly war thinking that he was coming home to a wife with whom he could settle down and raise the next generation of the Leybourne family.

*   *   *

The quarrel and the crying fit and her own guilty thoughts had left her feeling bleak and sick, and next morning, when a message came through to the ward that her mother-in-law was on the phone, Laura's empty feeling changed to one of doom. Jocelyn would only telephone if it was an emergency; was it Christopher or Nicholas, or had something happened to Jonathan?

'Jocelyn, are you all right?'

'Laura, there is a War Office letter for you, the postman has just brought it. Can you come home or shall I open it . . .? Laura, are you there?' Jocelyn was agitated and needed support, but Laura knew that it would be impossible to leave the busy ward.

'Jocelyn, I can't leave, it's absolutely hectic here. Will you open it? We can't wait until tonight.'

Laura could hear the rustle of paper, then there was silence.

'Jocelyn?'

Over the phone, Laura heard a half sob from Jocelyn. 'Oh, Laura, I can't read it. But Christopher is dead, Laura, and his grave is at El Alamein. Oh, Laura, I know we were prepared for it, but what shall we do? Can't you come home? Please try.'

Laura took a deep breath. 'Jocelyn, go and get Mrs Maw, I'll speak to her.' She felt numb, but realized that Jocelyn needed someone with her and who better than Mrs Maw?

She listened to the sound of the phone being put down and then there were voices and she heard Jonathan saying, 'Don't cry, Nana.'

Then the solid and sensible voice of Mrs Maw. 'I'm sorry, Miss Laura, I'm very sorry. Don't you worry about Mrs Leybourne, I'll see to her. You'll be that busy, just come as soon as you can.'

'Thank you, Mrs Maw, I'll see you at teatime.'

Laura turned from the phone, but didn't have a second in which to think; the whole of the rest of the day was very busy and Laura was glad. James did his round between further operations; there were drips and transfusions to see to as men returned from the operating theatre, and in between, the constant to and fro of getting patients out of bed to go for physiotherapy. Not once did she show any emotion or even think of Christopher, and so

240

the day went speedily by.

But she did manage to have a quick word with James before she left, and told him the news of Christopher.

He gripped her arm. 'I'm very sorry, Laura. Would you please tell Jocelyn that I will try and come later this evening to see her?'

'Oh, thank you, James; how can I thank you?'

'Off you go, I'll see you later.'

Once in her car, she was overcome by tiredness and the sense of numbness returned. It seemed almost as though nothing had changed; Christopher had come into her life and then gone out of it, all that was different was that she now knew that he would never come back.

She didn't even bother to put the car away, but hurried into the house to find Jocelyn. It was Jonathan who ran across the hall to meet her.

'Mummy . . . Daddy's not coming home any more; he's gone to Heaven and Nana's been crying. Are we going to have tea now, I'm hungry?'

She hugged the little boy and carried him into the drawing-room where she found Jocelyn sitting at the window. As soon as Jonathan had been old enough to understand, they had shown him pictures of Christopher, and Laura had felt the knife turn inside her every time she had explained to him about his daddy. Now it meant very little to him and she could understand it.

She bent down and kissed Jocelyn, who was looking pale and strained, but she tried to smile and Laura admired her courage when she spoke quietly. 'It's going to be a long time before I can really believe that we are never going to see him again. It's hard for me to lose a son, but it's worse for you to lose a husband, Laura.'

'It's strange, Jocelyn, it's just as though I was only meant to have those few days with Christopher and that I was never to know him properly. I can't feel, I can't cry. I'm sorry, you will think I'm unfeeling, but being a nurse brings you face to face with death almost every day. We see such bad injuries and can do nothing; we lost a young private today and I shall have to speak to his widow when she comes. I'm just another widow, a war widow. I'm afraid that there are thousands of us.'

Jocelyn looked at the young face, so serious and so accepting. 'Yet you are not bitter, Laura, why is that?'

Laura thought before she spoke. 'I'm not sure. I think it's because Hitler and all he stands for is an evil, and evil has to be overcome with good. If that means fighting and losing lives, then it is a sacrifice we all have to make; not just the men, but their families, too. We have to believe that we are going to win this war, Jocelyn, we have to believe that our country will not be invaded. We *are* winning, the news is good; we've got Rome back and that seems like a prize of war, but in order to gain prizes we lose something in the process. We have lost Christopher, you and I, but we are not going to lose the war.' She stopped speaking and looked at her mother-in-law. 'I'm sorry, I shouldn't go on like that, but I wanted you to know what I felt about it.'

'You are a dear, brave girl,' said Jocelyn. 'And thank heaven there are thousands like you. I won't weep any more, Laura; we have Jonathan and it is his future we must think of. After all, we are trying to make the world a better place for him, aren't we?'

The little boy had stayed quiet at his grandmother's side all this time, but as she finished speaking, he took her hand and pulled at it and said in a firm voice, 'And now it's teatime, isn't it, Nana?'

Laura and Jocelyn couldn't help laughing; it was almost a hysterical reaction and Jonathan, not knowing what it was all about, joined in, too. By the time they got to the kitchen, their spirits were restored and from that moment, their lives continued as before.

James came later in the evening, and Laura was not surprised to see him take Jocelyn into his arms and lay his cheek against her hair. No word was said, but there was understanding, thought Laura.

While James and Laura were talking, Laura had a surprise visit from Marcia who was still in her corduroys. They met in the courtyard.

'Laura, I'm not staying, for we haven't finished in New Furlong field yet, but I just had to come and say that I was sorry about Christopher. Jocelyn phoned me with the news at lunchtime. And, Laura, I'm sorry that we had that quarrel; perhaps you will be able to comfort Nicholas now, for I have not changed my mind. I love Ronald and I have promised him.'

Laura knew that it had cost Marcia a lot to apologize and she held out her hand. Marcia took it and Laura said very little. 'Thank you for coming, Marcia, it was nice of you and I don't want to quarrel, either. I do understand.'

Marcia got back into the farm truck and Laura watched her drive off. How is it all going to end, she thought? All that was left to them now was to wait for news of Nicholas. And she hoped with all her heart that they wouldn't be receiving another letter of the kind that had come that day.

Over the following months, there were landmarks in the fighting in Europe, and the spirits of the young men returning from France were running high. At the same time, the Germans had started to terrify London with the launch of the horrifying flying bombs, and it was not until the French sites were taken that the VI and V2 rockets ceased.

The Christmas holiday at Hayle was a happy one, in spite of the loss of Christopher and the lack of news from Nicholas. James was there with them as he had been the previous year and, as they were drinking their coffee after their Christmas dinner, James made the announcement that Laura had been expecting all year.

'My dear Laura,' he said solemnly. 'I would like you to know that Jocelyn has done me the honour of saying that she would like to become my wife . . . why are you laughing?'

For Laura had got up and kissed them both and could not stop her chuckles of laughter. 'I'm sorry, I do apologize, but I guessed as soon as you met last Christmas. I couldn't be happier for you both, but why have you waited all this time?'

They all laughed then and Jocelyn explained, 'You see, we can't be sure what is going to happen at Hayle; we waited and waited and then decided to make it official on the anniversary of our meeting. It was a happy day for me, Laura, when you brought your James to Hayle, and I am glad that you are pleased, I guessed you would be. We are not making any plans until we hear from Nicholas, but we thought it would be nice to get engaged on Christmas Day.'

Laura kissed her again and then tried to explain to Jonathan; it was a happy occasion for them all in spite of their sadness over

Christopher and the uncertain fate of Nicholas.

New Year 1945 dawned, and there was continuing good news from the Western Front with cheers going up in the ward every time another German town was captured. It was the day that Frankfurt fell which Laura was to remember.

When she got home from the hospital that night, it was to find Jocelyn on the steps of the front porch looking worried and anxious, with a serious-looking Jonathan holding her hand. Laura's heart sank, yet she did not think it could have been a War Office communication or Jocelyn would have phoned her on the ward.

She jumped out of the car.

'What is it, Jocelyn?' she cried out as she ran up the steps. 'What is wrong?'

'It's Nicholas, it's Nicholas,' was all Jocelyn could say; tears were streaming down her cheeks and she did not attempt to brush them away.

'Is he . . . is he dead?' Laura had to ask the question. But Jocelyn was incapable of speech and Laura followed her into the house. Jocelyn went into the drawing-room. Laura saw at once that they had a visitor; a tall, gaunt ill-looking man who was sitting on the sofa. He was so thin, he looked like a skeleton; his face was a yellowish brown, with the lines of an old man.

Laura stood there and he tried to get up, but he did not have the strength.

Then she found herself looking into dark eyes. He tried to speak.

'Laura,' his voice said, and she knew it.

It was Nicholas.

Laura stood as though she had been turned to a block of stone; she could not move, she could not speak. She saw the hair, still dark; she saw the eyes, but they were set in deep sunken sockets; his mouth was thin and twisted. It was the face of a stranger.

It was Jonathan who moved first.

He ran to the sofa and took Nicholas's hand. 'This is Niklas, Mummy; he is ill.' The little boy gazed at the still figure sitting there. 'You've got dark hair, like me. Nana's got white hair.'

Jocelyn was the next to take any action; she stepped forward, picked up Jonathan and then turned to Laura. 'Nicholas is home, Laura; I will take Jonathan and leave you together.'

As she heard the click of the door, Laura moved at last. She went up to the sofa as Jonathan had done and took Nicholas's hand in hers; his flesh felt dry and papery, she could feel the bones.

'Is it really you, Nicholas?' She spoke with a break in her voice. 'I'm sorry, I did not recognize you at first.'

'I don't blame you, Laura, it's like coming back from the dead; in fact, I think I have come back from the dead. It almost seems as though I have gone to Heaven being at Hayle again; and you are still here, Laura. You are here.'

The more he spoke and the more he looked at her, she could see the old Nicholas returning; he was here, he was alive. Reaching up, she gently touched the wasted cheek with her soft lips.

'Laura, oh Laura.' And Nicholas broke down and cried. It was fortunate that at that moment, the door opened again and Jocelyn came in carrying a tray of tea.

'We all need a cup of tea,' she said, and to Laura's delight she saw a smile come into Nicholas's face.

'Good old Mother,' he said. 'The days and months I've yearned to hear her say those very words.'

The hot drink seemed to give him a little strength and, when Jocelyn asked him if he could get as far as the kitchen, he took Laura's arm and shuffled through the hall, then sat down thankfully at the kitchen table.

He did eat something, but it seemed to exhaust him doing just that. 'I want to sleep,' he said. 'Just sleep and sleep; we've got days and weeks to talk. Laura, do you think you could help me upstairs?'

Laura became nurse then and got him undressed and into bed; he slept immediately, and suddenly, as she looked at his sleeping face, she could recognize the same, familiar Nicholas.

Downstairs, Jocelyn was on the phone. 'No, don't come tonight, he is asleep. Try and come tomorrow afternoon; he will be stronger then.' She rang off and turned to Laura. 'I've told Marcia and she will come tomorrow. He needs the rest. Oh, Laura.'

And suddenly, the two women were in each other's arms, giving way to emotion which had taken years to build up.

'What time did he come?' Laura asked. 'Did he send you no warning?'

'No, an ambulance brought him at about four o'clock. You didn't know him, did you, Laura? I don't think I would have done if he hadn't said "Hello, Mother".'

'Has he spoken to you at all? Do you know what has happened?'

'Only a few words,' Jocelyn replied. 'He fell asleep as soon as he sat down and when he woke up, he was so excited to find himself at Hayle. It was then I realized that it really was Nicholas. I told Jonathan that it was his Uncle Nicholas, but he could only manage "Niklas". I don't think it matters.'

'And what has he told you?'

'Only that he was in Burma and was taken prisoner by the Japanese. I think they starved him and then he got cholera; he's been in hospital in Rangoon, but he told them he was fit, so they sent him home.' Jocelyn looked at

Laura and her expression was a mixture of pride and pity. 'He's going to need a lot of nursing and feeding up, Laura.'

'Don't worry too much, Jocelyn,' Laura said gently. 'I think you will be surprised at how quickly he will pick up once we can get some good food into him. We've got him safely home, that is the most important thing.'

Laura worked the whole of the next day in a dream. James was pleased with her news, though he warned her that prisoners-of-war often suffer from a psychological reaction as well as a physical one.

When she pulled up at the front of the house that evening, she saw the farm truck and knew that Marcia must be there. At least she had the decency to come, Laura thought.

But as she opened the front door, she heard a raised voice coming from the direction of the drawing-room.

Laura had no intention of eavesdropping, but was mesmerized by the angry, strident voice of a Marcia who was obviously confronting Nicholas.

'Well, as I said, I'm sorry to see you like this, but I've got something to say and I'm losing no time. I've waited long enough. Our marriage was almost over before you went away and I certainly can't see myself being tied to an invalid for the rest of my life. I want you to divorce me. Yes, I've given you grounds because I've been living over at the farm with

Ronald and he wants to marry me as soon as possible. So, if you wouldn't mind getting your firm to put it in hand, I'd be very grateful. That's all I've got to say, except that I'll move all my stuff out tonight; there's not a lot here now. So, you won't see me again and you should get better soon with your mother and Laura to look after you. Goodbye, then.'

At these final words, Laura started to move, but not quickly enough. The door opened and Marcia nearly fell over her.

'So, you've been listening, have you, Laura? I'll leave Nicholas to your tender care.'

She ran upstairs, leaving Laura standing speechless; the bitch, she said to herself, the rotten, stinking bitch, telling Nicholas like that, when he's right down. How could she?

She went into the drawing-room to find Nicholas in the chair by the window, his head in his hands; she ran quickly over to him.

'Nicholas, Nicholas, how could she when you are so ill? She's a bitch, I could kill her.'

But she found Nicholas taking her hands and saying her name. 'Hush, Laura, it doesn't matter. I think I'm glad. Let her go; Ronald is welcome to her. As long as I've got you and Mother, I'll be all right.'

He held on to her tightly, his emaciated and haunted face tired and drained. She knew that she must forget her anger at Marcia and be the one to help him.

'Go and have a lie-down before supper,

251

Nicholas, I'll help you upstairs.'

'Wait till she's gone,' he whispered.

It was only minutes later that they heard the sound of the truck driving away and Laura got Nicholas to bed; they had put him into Christopher's old room to save him the extra staircase up to the flat.

Laura went in search of Jocelyn, who listened to what she had to say. 'So we've seen the last of Marcia,' was all the comment Jocelyn made, and she turned away.

Laura changed out of her uniform and tried to forget the ugly scene. Jonathan was full of chatter, and not for the first time Laura was glad to be distracted by him.

By the time Laura was due for her next two days off, Nicholas had improved a lot. His face had already lost its sunken look and was a better colour, and he was sleeping less during the day. He spent long hours sitting at the French windows of the drawing-room, staring down the back gardens of Hayle, over to the distant woods and hills. She had not had any long conversation with him and there was no repeat of the emotional scene after Marcia had left him. In fact, he seemed reserved, almost withdrawn.

The first of April dawned fine and sunny; the cold winds of March had disappeared and Laura, being home for a few days, wondered if she should suggest to Nicholas that he might like to sit outside on the terrace.

252

Jocelyn had found, stored safely away in the loft, a little old tricycle that had belonged to Christopher and Nicholas when they were small; she had kept it all those years and Jonathan loved it. He would ride round and round the terrace and up and down the garden path for hours, and was always disappointed and fractious if the day was too wet or too cold for him to go out.

So, on that fine April morning, Laura took him outside and then went back to speak to Nicholas; he was sitting in his usual place at the window and seemed to be watching Jonathan with a pleased expression.

'Nicholas, don't you think it's warm enough for you to sit out in the sun this morning? The fresh air would do you good.'

She was surprised when he gave a heavy frown; it was taut and nervous and his speech was hesitant.

'I don't know, Laura . . . I think I feel safer indoors . . . I like looking down the garden, you see.'

Problem number one, she said to herself. We are going to get a lot of this; his confidence is shattered.

She spoke carefully. 'We will just open the French windows and put the chairs outside in the sun; it's nice and sheltered there and it faces south. I'll sit with you, and we can watch Jonathan on his tricycle. I don't want to leave him out there on his own.'

He looked up at her and then out to the happy child. 'Yes . . . yes, Laura, we will just sit outside the window and you can talk to me. I've not seen a lot of you, for I'm usually asleep by the time you get back from the hospital.'

Victory, said Laura to herself, and unlocked the window and moved the chairs on to the terrace.

Jonathan waved from the garden path.

'Niklas!' he called out. 'Can you see me?'

'Yes, I've come out to watch you, Jonathan.' He sounded more cheerful and positive, then he turned to Laura sitting at his side. 'It's strange,' he said, 'I expected Jonathan to be a carbon copy of Christopher—fair hair and all—but he is dark, much more like me, isn't he?'

CHAPTER ELEVEN

Laura swallowed hard at Nicholas's comment. She must make herself accustomed to remarks like this and, every day seeing Nicholas and Jonathan together, seemed to make her self-imposed task more difficult.

She looked at him. 'Are you feeling a little better, Nicholas?'

'Yes, thank you, I think I feel stronger. Dr Ross said that it was mainly malnutrition and the effects of the cholera. I lived on rice for nearly a year.'

'Was that all you had?'

'It was; occasionally they would give us a bit of dried salt fish with the rice, but it was revolting. Then there was a shortage of water and what we did get wasn't pure, so the cholera epidemic started; thousands died, poor bastards. I clung on, thinking that the war in Burma would soon come to an end, but I was nearly done for when I was released. I used to think of you, Laura; the thought of you kept me going.'

Laura looked at him, it was the most he had spoken of his experiences since his return; perhaps it would do him good to talk about it all. She wondered if it was time to mention Marcia.

'I'm sorry about Marcia, Nicholas; I thought all would be well when the war was over.'

He shook his head. 'Things had started to go wrong, then we quarrelled on my last visit home; I knew she was spending a lot of time with Ronald. I forgot her, it was strange, I never thought about her at all. It was you I thought of, and how we used to sit on the seat in the wood and look across the dale; it seemed as though I had a picture in front of me. I didn't even feel guilty about it; I knew that I couldn't marry you, but all that didn't seem to come into it. As long as I could imagine you, I was all right; you were like a talisman to me.'

'Your lucky charm, Nicholas.' Laura tried to joke, she didn't want to be drawn into a serious conversation.

'I'm sorry about Christopher, Laura; what a good job you've got Jonathan to think about. He's a blessing to Mother, too, isn't he?'

'Yes, there's a lot of love on both sides there. Your mother has been marvellous, Nicholas. Looking after Jonathan so that I could go back to nursing; I felt I had to go, it seemed such a waste not to.'

'Yes, I understand.' He was smiling and she turned to see Jonathan leave his trike and come to stand by Nicholas's side.

'Would Niklas play football like James?'

Nicholas turned to Laura. 'What does he mean?'

Laura laughed. 'He loves kicking a ball in the garden. But we haven't told you about James yet. He is Mr Greenway, the surgeon at the hospital, and I invited him here for Christmas dinner over a year ago; he and Jocelyn fell for one another! They got engaged this Christmas, but a wedding hasn't been planned yet. They were waiting until you came home.'

'Mother to be married again? That's wonderful news; I am so pleased for her and I look forward to meeting this James. Mother has gone through so much but it's been a hard war for you, too, Laura. I think sometimes

256

when we are posted abroad, or get shot down, or taken prisoner, that we are the only sufferers. But those left at home suffer, too, don't they?'

He reached across and took her hand and Laura gladly held on to him; it seemed a natural gesture and she was hoping that the conversation was helping him. 'Shall we go in now? I think that's enough for the first time out.'

But Nicholas was looking at Jonathan who was still standing there expectantly. 'Jonathan, I'm afraid I can't play football yet, but would you like to take me for a walk as far as the shrubbery and back? I'll hold your hand and you can help me along.'

Laura watched them go and felt like crying; Nicholas was walking but haltingly, and Jonathan, carefully and protectively, held on to his hand. They are father and son, she almost cried it out loud, what have I done? Whatever have I done? And what am I going to do? There seemed to be no answer and she busied herself taking the chairs back indoors; by the time that was done, the two of them were back again and she had regained her composure.

April passed quickly; Easter came and went and the days lengthened. Nicholas made good progress and sat outside for most of the day when it was fine; he now had a healthy-looking tan and had started to put on weight. Jocelyn and Mrs Maw were determined to feed him well, and were helped by kind gifts of chicken, eggs and pieces of pork from Ronald. They heard nothing of Marcia and the divorce was almost through.

Laura was happy to see Nicholas improving, but noticed that he did not again speak of his experiences under the Japanese. She hoped that it was all slipping into the back of his mind.

By the end of the month, everything was forgotten in the excitement of the news coming out of Germany and Italy. Mussolini had been captured, and from that time on every day seemed to bring fresh hopes of an imminent victory. Hitler's death was announced by Hamburg radio on 1 May, and the following day Berlin surrendered; Laura was on days and the excitement on the ward was intense. A few days later, all German forces surrendered to Field Marshal Montgomery: the war in Europe had ended.

Laura couldn't wait to get home. She arrived at the front of Hayle House to find Bates putting flags over the front porch and Nicholas holding on to the ladder. Jonathan was running madly up and down the garden waving a Union Jack; not knowing what it was all about, he had nonetheless caught the mood of the moment and Laura afterwards wondered if he would remember that day. He was almost three years old.

She got out of the car and ran up to them. Bates climbed down the ladder and gave her a kiss, Nicholas caught her in his arms and held her tight; she lifted her head with shining eyes, then felt the gentle touch of his lips on hers.

'Laura, it's victory,' he cried. 'At last, at long last. Only the Japs to finish off now.'

Jocelyn came out of the house at all the noise and there were more hugs and kisses. 'We're celebrating,' she said. 'Nicholas has found champagne in the cellar and I've got a chicken roasting. It won't be long. Go and get changed, Laura; put on your prettiest dress and give James a ring; tell him to come out as soon as he can.'

Then, while the washing-up was hastily done, Bates disappeared into the garden and came back a short while later to announce that he had built a bonfire. As it was in the middle of the vegetable plot, they felt it was an honour; he said he had been saving all the dry stuff for a long time. By the time they had sung 'God Save the King' and 'Auld Lang Syne', Laura could see that Nicholas was beginning to look tired and she ushered them all back into the house, where she got Jonathan to bed while Mrs Maw and Jocelyn made coffee.

They listened to Mr Churchill's victory broadcast to the nation and their spirits could not be dampened when he gave his warning:

. . . that there is still a lot to do, and that

259

you must be prepared for further efforts
of mind and body and further sacrifices
to great causes . . .

Then, to Nicholas's satisfaction came the
important words:

I cannot tell you tonight how much or
what exertions will be required to compel
the Japanese to make amends for their
odious treachery and cruelty.

Nicholas was crying quite openly and Laura
caught his hand. 'He hasn't forgotten,' he
sobbed. 'We thought he had forgotten us.'
Then he looked at Laura. 'I'm sorry, my dear;
would you like a walk in the garden?'
'Are you sure you are not too tired?' she
asked him.
'Not today,' he told her and smiled. 'I would
like to go down to the wood with you, Laura,
there is no need to hurry. I've been looking
forward to going there and today seems the
right day.' And then he suddenly gave a
mischievous grin. 'I think we can safely leave
Mother with James, don't you?'
She put on a cardigan and Nicholas
discarded his sports jacket for a thick jersey;
he was still so thin that he looked lost in it, but
Laura felt pleased that he felt relaxed enough
to wear it.
Although he was calm, Laura found that he

held her hand tightly and walked as though each step was an effort.

'Do you think I will ever recover, Laura?' he asked, as they reached the seat and he sank down thankfully. 'Even a walk like that seems to take it out of me.'

'It's early days, Nicholas; you mustn't forget that your muscles were wasted and you were half starved; you can't expect to regain your old strength in a matter of weeks.'

'You are right, sweet Laura, I must be thankful to be back at Hayle with you and Mother. I've got a lot to look forward to, for in a few months I'll be able to take up the reins of the estate. Reggie Peacock and Tom Hird have done so well in my absence; I think that those who have been left behind in this country must have doubled their workload, the farms have become so important to us.' He looked at her. 'And you, Laura, working so hard at the hospital. How long will you stay there?'

She was silent at his question; her future was a total blank to her and she could think only as far as the next day.

'I don't know, Nicholas. Without Christopher, I will have to support myself and Jonathan, and I cannot expect your mother to go on looking after him indefinitely; soon she and James will be married and things will change.' She looked across at him. 'I have taken it for granted that you would let me stay at Hayle for the time being, but you may want to make changes. I could always get accommodation for myself and Jonathan somewhere in the garrison.'

But Nicholas was indignant. 'Jonathan's place is at Hayle and he is staying here. Now that everything is finished with Marcia, I want him to grow up loving the place just as Christopher and I did.'

'But, Nicholas, you might marry again one day.'

'Never,' he said shortly. 'Marcia has finished me as far as marriage is concerned. What is more to the point, Laura, is that you might marry again. You've only got to have a handsome doctor come along and you'll be off!'

She laughed then and was pleased to hear him join in; to hear Nicholas laugh was very rare.

'I don't think it likely, somehow.' She got up. 'It's time we were walking back; it's beginning to get chilly.'

'I'm glad we came, Laura; I often thought of this view when I was in Burma, we were in the jungle, you know . . .' He broke off. 'But I don't want to remind myself of that tonight. I was glad that Churchill didn't forget, though . . . "odious treachery and cruelty" he called it, and he was right. But today is for rejoicing. I am sure we will win in the East just as we have done in Germany.' He stood up; he seemed taller than ever, Laura thought, as she stood by his side. 'Do I get a celebratory kiss, Laura?'

She was standing within the circle of his arms and with a smile she laid her head against the wool of his jersey. He gently turned her face up to his and his lips touched her forehead and her cheek; she offered her mouth and in the gentleness of the kiss, she felt some of their old magic. The contact was thrilling and she put her arms round his neck and whispered her words.

'It's lovely to have you home, Nicholas.'

'It's lovely to be home, Laura.'

The walk back to the house was slow and the light was fading; the enclosed garden was sheltered and friendly and Laura felt that was just how her relationship with Nicholas was. She would help him all she could and not think of tomorrow.

*   *   *

Towards the end of the summer came the end of the war against Japan. Laura felt ill with a sick and sinking horror when she heard that an atom bomb had been dropped over Hiroshima and she learned of the terrible effects on the population of that city. She went home from the hospital and sought out Nicholas and he took her in his arms.

'It is so terrible, Nicholas, it is indescribable. Was it necessary, was it really necessary?'

'Hush, Laura, don't cry; it will bring the war

263

to a quick conclusion, and that is the most important thing.'

Three days later, the second bomb was dropped, on Nagasaki, and a stunned world could scarcely rejoice when the Japanese accepted the Allied terms and surrendered.

The defeat of the Japanese had a strange effect on Nicholas. Outwardly, he was fit and slowly putting on weight; Dr Ross was satisfied with his progress and stopped his weekly visits. Yet Laura knew that all was not well. On the surface, he was cheerful, he ate well and he was devoted to Jonathan who followed him around as though Nicholas was a playmate of his own age. It amused Laura to see them together, yet at the same time it disturbed her conscience and she could see no solution to the dilemma in which she had placed herself.

It was the look in Nicholas's eyes which worried her: he often looked tired and hollow-eyed. He never mentioned his experiences and she wondered if it would help him to talk about it more, but she seemed to lack the courage to ask him, and let the days drift by hoping that time would indeed be the healer.

But by the beginning of September, a real concern for Nicholas seized Laura and she knew she would have to act soon. She hardly spoke to him and he had taken to going to the upstairs flat in the evenings after dinner; it seemed that he was becoming more and more depressed and withdrawn as each day passed.

In the end, it was Nicholas who approached her and in a way which was to startle her. She still occupied the big double bedroom she had shared with Christopher. Jonathan had a small room across the corridor.

That day, she had been very busy on the ward, and when Nicholas had hardly spoken at dinner-time, she had been too tired to take a lot of notice and concentrated on her evening game with Jonathan and then the child's bath and bedtime. It was a fine evening. Nicholas disappeared upstairs as usual, and she walked down the garden to try and relax before going to bed; there would be another busy day tomorrow.

Her nightdress on and her hair loose, she sat on her bed for a few moments, thinking yet again of Nicholas and of what she could do to help him. A sound made her look up and she saw the door being opened slowly and quietly. Nicholas let himself into the room; he was in his pyjamas and a dressing-gown of deep red; he looked ill.

'Nicholas.' Laura stood up and put out a hand to him. 'What is it?'

'Laura, I've got to talk to you. I must talk to someone. Forgive me coming to you like this. I think I am going mad, Laura.'

'Nicholas.' She led him to the bed and they sat down side by side.

'I've been trying to pluck up the courage to come and ask you.'

'What do you want to ask me?' she said quietly.

'If you say no, I don't know what I shall do.' He sounded desperately nervous and shaky. 'Laura, I want to ask you if I could come and talk to you at bedtime until I can get to sleep.'

She turned and looked at him; there was pity and tenderness in her eyes, and she knew that she would do anything to help him.

He went on speaking. 'It's sleep, Laura, I can't sleep. And I keep having the feeling that if only you were near to me, if I was able to talk to you about what I went through, then I would be able to sleep.'

Laura felt as though the power of speech had been completely taken away from her. He was in a worse state than she had imagined; but she must try and be practical. He really needed professional help: would she be able to supply the need?

'Nicholas, why can't you sleep? You slept so much when you first came home. What has happened?'

His voice sounded strange. 'When I first came back, I was exhausted, too exhausted even to think, all I wanted was sleep. But as time has gone on and I've got better, it all keeps coming back to me; it goes over and over in my mind and I can't stop it. All night long, I'm tossing and turning and thinking and thinking. If only I could talk to someone about it all; I suppose I should see a psychiatrist, but

I'd rather talk to you, Laura. I'd rather talk to you than anyone else in the world. Will you listen to me, Laura, or is it too much to ask after a hard day's work?'

Then she behaved as though she were being directed from a long way off; she lay down on the bed and made room for him by her side. Without saying a word and still in his dressing-gown, he lay down beside her and threw an arm around her waist.

'Nicholas, tell me.'

But then he could not speak, he pulled close to her, buried his face in her neck and wept. Great, deep, heaving sobs which frightened her.

'Nicholas, you must tell me,' she tried again.

'Oh, Laura, I've always thought that I was such a strong person. In the camp, lots of them gave in and they were the ones who died first. There were cremations every day and they made us make little boxes for the ashes. Then, the next day we had to dig great holes in the ground, big enough for a body, but they only put the little boxes in and then we had to throw the soil on top. I keep thinking of it; every day was the same; living skeletons we were and treated like animals. In the mornings, when we woke up, there were always some who had given up and died in the night and it started all over again . . .'

He stopped and gave a shudder.

'Go on,' Laura said, as her arms tightened

about him.

'I tried to think of you, and I thought of Hayle, I tried to fill my mind with good thoughts. I wouldn't give in. But that's what I see now when I should be sleeping, living skeletons digging their own graves, with those devils looking on, taunting and sneering, ready with the stick or the whip if we paused for more than a second. And then the next day gone, no life, nothing left except for a few ashes.'

Laura whispered, 'Nicholas, just hold on to me and shut your eyes and remember that for all their sufferings those poor soldiers are now at rest. Their suffering is over and yours must be, too.'

There was a long silence and Laura did not know what to say or do. Then Nicholas suddenly got out of the bed and stood looking down at her. 'Laura,' he said hoarsely, 'I think I love you. Thank you, my darling girl, I will go back to my own bed now. I will be able to sleep.'

Laura felt exhausted, but she had her reward, for she slept and the next night after dinner, Nicholas stayed and played with Jonathan in the garden and did not disappear up to the flat as he had been doing.

When they sat down with their books and the wireless, Nicholas looked across at her; they were on their own in the drawing-room at that moment.

'Laura, how can I thank you? I've felt so different today, but what about you, it's not fair on you, is it?'

She smiled. 'Don't worry about me, Nicholas, I had been so worried about you and it's a relief to know what was wrong. You need to talk about it, don't you? I should have asked you before, I blame myself.'

'No, never that, Laura, but I've got to ask you. Can I come to you again, just for a few more nights? I think it will do the trick.'

She had to say yes; how could she refuse him? Perhaps he needed the physical contact, too.

'Yes, Nicholas, you can come to me if it will help you, but I want you to promise me something first.' She was suddenly confident and knew the direction to go. 'I want you to promise to talk to me whenever you feel the need; tell me what haunts you most, tell me about the Japanese, the hardships, everything that happened. It's all over now; you are safely home; you can't let it worry you for the rest of your life.'

It was not difficult to get him to talk; words came pouring out and she learned of the terrible conditions in the camp; she learned of those who tried to escape into the jungle and were executed; she also learned to listen without taking it all too much to heart, just to let Nicholas slowly get it out of his system.

In the weeks that followed, Laura was

astonished at Nicholas's recovery; but no sooner was that crisis over and Nicholas returned to his old energetic self, when Laura seemed to be faced with another one and this time she felt herself quite unable to cope with it. For, as Jonathan grew older, he became more and more attached to Nicholas. To the little boy, 'Niklas' was the centre of his world and the two of them did everything together, whether it was playing football or going for walks.

She still worked at the garrison hospital and had been promised by Matron that the job would continue, even though the war was over. Coming home one evening to find Nicholas in a non-smiling and strange mood, she felt dismay as well as tiredness. Was he being bothered by sleeplessness again, she wondered? He had been so much better lately.

When Jonathan had gone to bed and Jocelyn was in her own sitting-room, Nicholas told Laura he wanted to talk to her. She thought he sounded odd, but not in the same stressful way as previously.

All was quiet in the drawing-room, and suddenly Nicholas put his hand in his pocket and held out a piece of card to Laura; it was a photograph.

She looked at it and smiled. 'Why, Nicholas, it's a photograph of Jonathan. Whenever was that taken?'

Nicholas was staring at her and she felt

uncomfortable. Whatever was wrong?

'Laura Leybourne, that is not a photograph of Jonathan, it is one taken of me when I was the same age. I found it this morning in a box of Mother's. You immediately thought it was Jonathan, but it is of me. Are you going to explain that to me?'

Laura felt herself go hot and then cold; she knew she must be as white as a sheet. She was still staring at the picture, realizing as she did so that the child was dressed in the clothes of an earlier generation; at first, she had only looked at the bright little smile and the dark hair and eyes. She knew then that the time had come for honesty, but she was in the grip of fear, unable to move, almost unable to speak.

'Well, Laura, have you nothing to say?' Nicholas's voice was edged with a note of scepticism and scorn.

'I'm sorry, Nicholas, I should have told you before.' She jerked the words out and did not look at him.

'Told me *what* before?' Nicholas was not going to make it easy for her.

'Jonathan is your son.'

The words dropped between them into a dreadful silence, then Nicholas got up and stood by the French windows, staring into the garden.

'I'm sorry, Nicholas.' She said it yet again and then he was turning back to her and towering over her.

'Are you telling me that Jonathan is my son and not Christopher's, that he was born as a result of that night we spent together after the air-raid in London?'

'Yes.'

'And you have let me go on thinking all this time that he was Christopher's son?'

'Yes.'

The next words were explosive. 'And what if Christopher had returned thinking the child was his? Would you never have told me the truth? Would you have let me live the rest of my life not knowing that I had a son? What have you to say to all that, Laura?'

By now, Laura was close to tears under the aggressive onslaught of his words. This was the savage anger she had feared from Nicholas.

'My God, Laura, how could you do it? I would never have believed it possible that you could be capable of such deceit and treachery. I have always admired you so much; I thought I loved you, and now this.' He stopped speaking and stood fiercely glaring at her. 'You have very little to say.'

A hot bubble of anger suddenly dissipated the threat of tears and Laura found herself shouting back, 'You are not thinking of me at all, it is all your wounded pride. How could I have told you? How could I have told Christopher that I had been unfaithful to him with his own brother and then that the child whom he thought of as his son was not his own? Have you thought of the position I was in? I didn't go into it lightly, I spent hours thinking of what to do for the best; I always thought that you would come back to Marcia and that you would have other sons of your own and that it wouldn't matter—'

He interrupted her with a violent laugh. 'It wouldn't matter that I had a son of my own? You must be mad. I'll never trust you again, Laura; I've no wish ever to speak to you again. I cannot forgive what you have done . . . Laura.'

But Laura had rushed from the room; she could bear to hear no more and she ran and ran until she had reached the wood and the sanctuary of the seat. She had lost Nicholas's love for ever; her heart felt like stone, but she could not cry.

*   *   *

Back at the house, Nicholas went in search of his mother; he guessed that she would be in the small sitting-room next to her bedroom where she liked to be quiet sometimes.

She was startled when he burst into the room. 'Nicholas, whatever is it? I have never seen you looking so angry.'

'I *am* angry, Mother, I am also shocked. Did you know that Jonathan is my child and not Christopher's?'

Jocelyn swallowed hard; the truth was out

273

and she guessed that he and Laura had quarrelled.

'It was not hard to imagine after you showed me that old photograph you had found; in any case, I think I knew from the very start. She was very sickly the last time Christopher was here, then Dr Ross said that she'd got her dates wrong, and a perfectly healthy baby was born a full month early.' She looked at him and saw that he was listening intently. 'It is only recently that I have thought that Laura was wrong not to tell you, and now you have found out. Don't be angry with her, Nicholas, these things happen in wartime. Go and talk it over sensibly.'

'She's run off in a temper . . .' he started to say. 'Can you think where she would have gone, Mother?'

'I should think she must have run straight down to the wood and you will probably find her on the seat, Nicholas.'

He had bent and given her a hug. 'You are right, I will go after her. We can't ruin Jonathan's life because of a misunderstanding between us.'

On the edge of the wood, Laura, still wrapped up in misery, became aware of footsteps on the woodland path; she stiffened.

Then Nicholas was standing in front of her.

They stared at each other, but neither made a move.

A tear trickled down Laura's cheek and

274

Nicholas saw it. He held out his arms.

Without knowing she had moved, Laura found herself in his embrace; he said her name over and over again and then he kissed her. It was not one of the more gentle kisses she had been receiving since his return, it was the deep and passionate first kiss of the London air-raid.

Laura returned it and knew that the old Nicholas had come back to her, and she guessed that he loved her as she loved him.

He told her so. 'I love you, Laura, I love you. I loved you from the start, never knowing that you would be mine; and that night we spent together, the night that made Jonathan who he is, it remained in my memory all the time I was a prisoner. Without that memory, I don't think I would have survived to see you—and Jonathan—ever again. Will you forgive my anger with you just now?' He paused. 'What is it, my love?'

'No, Nicholas, you have to forgive me. I know it was wrong of me not to tell you, but you know how racked with dreadful memories you were when you returned; you were not ready for the news I had to tell you. I love you, too, you know.'

'What about Christopher?'

She gave a little smile. 'Christopher and I were thrown together by war, and I was very fond of him; it was foolish of me to marry him, but you know how persuasive he could be. It

275

was all done in fun and now we have lost him; can we make it up to him by forgiving each other?'

He sat her on the seat again. 'All is forgiveness and now you will marry me, won't you? But I'm not waiting for any ceremony. We will go back to tell Mother that all is well between us, and then I am coming to your room with a sane and glad heart; and I will make love to you all night long so that we can be sure that Jonathan will soon have a brother . . .'

'Or maybe a sister,' said Laura happily as he kissed her again.

*　　　*　　　*

Laura and Nicholas were married a month later in the little church at Marske; and it was a double wedding, for James and Jocelyn became man and wife at the same time. It had been happily agreed that Jocelyn and her new husband would live in James's Richmond house when he was on duty and that the flat at Hayle House would be theirs on his days off.

Laura's parents came for the wedding and so did her sister Dorothy, now back in London with a young family. Peace had been made with Ronald and Marcia, and they came to the church and to the reception afterwards; Rob and Meg managed to get down from Scotland and it was a happy occasion.

276

Nicholas was in his element managing the Hayle estate, and Laura left the hospital as soon as they could replace her. Jonathan started school in Richmond when he was four years old; he never called his father anything but 'Niklas', but always referred to him as 'my daddy'. Nine months later, another son was born to them and they called him Christopher; their family was completed with a little girl two years later.

Nicholas was in his room managing the
Aristocrats, and Laura whispered a question, as they could remove her. Jonathan
said Jonathan in kindhood what he was and
were still he came called his father the boy
had nights, but always referred to him as my
daddy. Mrs. smiled a little, and her she was
born to them and they called him Christopher
that family was completed with a little girl
years later.

We hope you have enjoyed this Large Print book. Other Chivers Press or Thorndike Press Large Print books are available at your library or directly from the publishers.

For more information about current and forthcoming titles, please call or write, without obligation, to:

Chivers Large Print
published by BBC Audiobooks Ltd
St James House, The Square
Lower Bristol Road
Bath BA2 3BH
UK
email: bbcaudiobooks@bbc.co.uk
www.bbcaudiobooks.co.uk

OR

Thorndike Press
295 Kennedy Memorial Drive
Waterville
Maine 04901
USA
www.gale.com/thorndike
www.gale.com/wheeler

All our Large Print titles are designed for easy reading, and all our books are made to last.